A
Harlequin
Romance

OTHER
Harlequin Romances
by LILIAN PEAKE

A SENSE OF BELONGING

by

LILIAN PEAKE

HARLEQUIN BOOKS   TORONTO
WINNIPEG

Original hard cover edition published in 1974
by Mills & Boon Limited.

SBN 373-01778-2

Harlequin edition published May 1974

Printed in Canada

CHAPTER ONE

THE girl's voice, resonant and vibrating, rang round the hall, and mingled, pure gold, with the evening sun flooding in through the windows. The audience, captivated by the performance, had forgotten the outside world.

The girl, with her youth, which contrasted so strongly with the listeners' advanced years, and her vitality, so evident for all that it was restrained and tamed, was reaching out to them with the purity of her voice and the stirring message in her words. She had mesmerised them, as she always did, moving them so deeply that they responded without reserve.

One or two were unashamedly crying, others were dabbing at their eyes. The song was over, the last notes died away. There was an intense silence, then the applause broke out.

The girl, her face flushed, rose from her chair, smiled and bowed. Holding her guitar under her arm, she made for a white-haired man sitting at the back of the hall. She had been singing to him.

The old man's face, grooved by the passage of years, lit up at her approach. He was no relative of hers, just a friend she had made as a result of her visits to this old people's club. As she stood at his side, others patted her on the back, their eyes still nostalgic with the memories she had aroused, and murmured their thanks.

"Come again, dear," they said, "come again."

She nodded and smiled, waiting until they had passed. Then she asked, "Are you ready to go now, Mr. de Verrier?"

He stood, straightening himself slowly as if there were a stiffness in his limbs, a stiffness which, for all his accumulated years, he was determined to overcome. "That's very kind of you, Carina, my dear," he said.

They went outside and the old man eased himself awkwardly into the white sports car. As he settled himself down, he seemed a little embarrassed, as if such luxury was not really his due. He waited, with the unquestioning patience of the elderly, while she fixed the roof into position. She knew that without its protection, the wind would whip through his sparse white hair and rob his lungs of breath.

Carina pulled up outside his house. It was semi-detached and modest-looking, with a small front garden full of the fragrant flowers of late summer. With some surprise, Carina saw a large red car occupying the driveway into which she usually turned.

"Have you a visitor, Mr. de Verrier?" she asked as she helped him unwind from the low-slung sports car.

He sighed, as if relieved to find himself in one piece on the pavement. "Not really a visitor, lass. It's my grandson."

As she turned from locking her car, her eyes lifted involuntarily and caught a vague glimpse of a face which appeared for a few seconds at an upstairs window. It was a glimpse so swift it told her nothing at all about its owner.

Carrying her guitar, Carina walked along the garden path by the old man's side, slowing her footsteps to match his. It was taken for granted that she would go in with him. The front door was on the catch and he pushed at it, stepping back with a courtesy which came from a different age, allowing her to enter the house in front of him.

As he followed her into the living-room, he explained the

6

grandson's presence. "The lad got himself a job in the neighbourhood, so I asked him to come and live with me. After all, I've enough empty rooms for a family to fill, let alone one grandson." He lowered himself into an armchair. "It'll be company for me. I was a bit lonely, Carrie." No one but he called her that. "It's nice for us old ones to have youngsters like you and him around."

"Youngster", "lad"? It sounded as if the young man must be in his teens. He was probably starting his first job.

The room felt stuffy, so Carina opened a window, making sure there was no draught blowing on to the old man. The floor was scattered with an assortment of objects, so she picked them up. He must have dropped them after the lady help had gone. The woman, who came in each day, cooked for him and looked after him. She was generally much too fussy to have overlooked such untidiness.

Carina thought, "If the grandson is a friendly sort, and likes our kind of music, I might persuade him to join our group."

"Cup of tea, Mr. de Verrier?" she asked, making for the door. This was something else she always did, but this evening he called her back. "Plenty of time for that. Sing to me first, lass. I keep thinking about the old days and the songs we used to sing when my wife was alive and the children were small."

He indicated a well-worn footstool and she sat on it obligingly, never minding his requests for her to sing to him.

"What shall it be, Mr. de Verrier?" Her voice softened. "What about *Songs my mother taught me*?"

He settled back in his armchair. "You know it's one of my favourites, Carrie." He looked at her with a moment's anxiety. "Would it upset you to sing it?"

She knew the reason for his question and shook her head. She tuned her guitar and closed her eyes. There were footsteps moving about in the room overhead, but as soon as

7

she started singing, they stopped.

Her voice rose and welled out, full and sweet, shedding some of its beauty like reflected sunlight on to the homely objects in the small, unpretentious room. As she enunciated the words, clearly and with loving precision, she infused into them a sadness and a depth of feeling which seemed to spring from a boundless and unfulfilled longing inside her. She sang,

> Songs my mother taught me
> In the days long vanish'd,
> Seldom from her eyelids
> Were the teardrops banish'd.
>
> Now I teach my children
> Each melodious measure,
> Oft the tears are flowing,
> Oft they flow from my mem'ry's treasure.

At the end there were tears in the singer's eyes as well as those of her listener, and the silence that followed was filled, not with applause, but with a sigh of contentment. To the singer it was thanks enough.

Something made her tense and look up. The old, primitive instinct had come into play, the instinct that warns of impending danger. She was being watched. But the stranger standing in the doorway was no dangerous animal stalking its prey – he was as human as she was – but he was staring at her with an intensity that made her prickle.

The silence grew so long – the old man's back was turned to the newcomer and therefore he could not see him – Carina had time to take in the height of the man, the obstinate squareness of his jaw and the disturbingly analytical eyes. His hair was dark and tended to fall across his forehead and there was a look about him of a self-sufficiency so complete it amounted almost to arrogance, so well-established it must have been deliberately cultivated over the years.

8

And yet there was in his face a sensitivity and a deep intelligence which, together with an unmistakable compassion in those keen eyes, would have confounded anyone who tried to brand him as hard and intractable.

Transfixed, Carina whispered, "Mr. de Verrier," trying with desperate politeness to draw the old man's attention to the stranger.

Her host levered himself up and turned slowly in his chair. "I knew it!" he chuckled, relaxing again. "I knew it would bring him down." He slapped the arm of the chair. "That's why I did it, that's why I asked you to sing." He raised his arm in a beckoning motion. "Come in, come in, Marcus. Can't resist the sound of music, can you, whatever form it might take, whether it's a record, a piano or a sweet young voice."

Was this, Carina thought, the "youngster", the "lad" to whom Mr. de Verrier had been referring? No teenager this, but a mature adult, and from the look of him, a world apart from hers.

The stranger entered slowly, as if reluctant to comply with his grandfather's request. He stood, one hand in his pocket, the other at his side, openly studying the girl who sat, guitar across her lap, gazing up at him with an expression which, judging by his frown, appeared to puzzle him. There was an unconscious pleading in her eyes, a frantic appeal, like a cry from a locked room, "Like me, please like me!"

He saw the jet black hair framing her face, the wide inviting mouth and the enormous brown eyes. Round her throat there was a chunky pure gold necklace, on her wrist a gold bracelet. He noted the careless but costly mode of dress – white heavily embroidered peasant-type blouse, impeccably cut red velvet trousers, short matching velvet waistcoat, sandals which seemed to consist only of soles and a couple of straps. And last of all his eyes came to rest on the scintillating solitaire diamond ring on the third finger of her hand. That it was intended to be an engagement ring could surely not be disputed, but for some reason best known to herself, it adorned the right hand, not the left.

Affluence, breeding and ease of living were manifest in her whole bearing and his reaction to the girl and everything she stood for was, it seemed, instant and automatic. Totally and unequivocally, he rejected her.

She saw with dismay the dismissal in his eyes and her inherent need to be approved of and well regarded became even more pronounced. She rose and thrust her outstretched hand towards him with an urgency which almost commanded him to place his in its grasp.

But he held back, it seemed deliberately, and she could not hide the disappointment his action aroused. He must, her expression said, accept her for what she was, and not reject her for what she seemed to be. He could not, surely, dislike her on sight?

Something, a response which must have escaped his rigid control, made him raise his hand at last and take hers, but the speed with which he withdrew it told her that he had erected a wall between them and that nothing she could say or do would break it down.

"Mr. de Verrier?" she asked, a smile, sweet and disarming, lighting up her eyes.

He inclined his head, failing completely to respond to the smile. "Marcus de Verrier. And you –?"

"She's Carina," his grandfather supplied. "Carrie to me."

"Just – Carina?" His voice was cool, cultured and toneless.

Her eyes lost their light and clouded over. She said flatly, "Everyone calls me Carina, but if you like you can call me Miss Ascott." She turned away.

Ernest de Verrier laughed at her reversal of the usual invitation to informality. But the grandson replied, his tone as indifferent as hers, "Miss Ascott it shall be."

. She turned back to search his face again. He narrowed his eyes, full of suspicion and mistrust, until they were no more than slits. He plainly resented her scrutiny. She was thinking, had the name meant nothing to him? But what would he know of the world of women's fashions? And even if he did – even if he had a wife – he probably would not have associated the name Ascott with that of the manufacturer of women's clothes of high quality and international repute. And that manufacturer was her father.

The name "Ascott" carried with it such distinction and was so prized by women that they had been known to carry their coats over their arms with the label revealed for envious eyes to see.

"Sit down, Marcus," Ernest invited. "It's your home now as well as mine."

Marcus selected a chair as far away as possible from his grandfather's guest. He eyed the guitar she was nursing with an interest far greater than he had shown in its owner.

"Did you hear her sing?" Ernest asked. Marcus nodded. "What did you think of it, eh? Marvellous, isn't she, marvellous!"

There was no reply. Instead, Marcus de Verrier extended his hand towards the guitar. "May I, Miss Ascott?" He forced a smile to go with his request.

Her response was so totally unexpected it astounded him. She pressed the instrument against her body like a child protecting a precious possession from an interfering, too inquisitive adult. He was so surprised he laughed and his face lost its austerity and came alive, adding another dimension – humanity – to his handsome, fine-drawn features.

"You can trust me, Miss Ascott. I promise not to maltreat your treasure."

Despite his reassurance, she still hesitated. In the end he rose and stood in front of her. Since it became obvious that she would not voluntarily give up the guitar, he removed it from her hands with the gentleness of a doctor taking a sick baby from the arms of an anguished mother.

"You can relax," he said, smiling. "I'm no vandal. I

11

recognise – and respect – a valuable possession when I see one."

He examined the guitar, turning it round and noting its quality. He sat sideways on the table, holding the guitar like an expert and resting it on his knee. His fingers ran over the strings, producing a few bars of classical music. He made an excellent sound, handling the instrument as if he were born to it.

"Can you play?" Carina was astonished by his apparent expertise, and that so studious a type of man with so distant and unbending a manner should know how to handle – and to play – such a thing as a guitar.

"The answer, Miss Ascott," he replied a little absently, his attention still on the guitar, "is that I can, I know how to, but I don't."

He gave her a quick, absorbed smile, his fingers stroking the strings, his mind centred on the sound which came from them. Her disappointment penetrated his concentration. "Sorry," he said, still smiling – not, she knew, at her but at the music his long sensitive fingers were feeling and enticing out of the guitar, as though every single note held a fascination for him.

"Sing to him, Carrie," Ernest pleaded.

The frown, which seemed never to be far from her face, returned. Her hand reached out uncertainly for the guitar, but Marcus held it back. Her outstretched fingers stiffened, desperate now as a hungry child after food. Was he tantalising her? What was his motive?

"Can't you sing without it, Miss Ascott?"

"No, it's impossible."

"Try."

"No, no . . . I must have it in my hands."

"Why?"

"I don't know why. I only know I must."

"Give it to her, Marcus. Taking away her guitar is like – like taking the seat from under someone."

"So it's her support, is it, her crutch?" To Carina,

12

Marcus said, "You should try to do without it. Go on, Miss Ascott, sing."

She looked horrified. "Sing – unaccompanied? But that's supposed to be one of the most difficult things for a singer to do."

"It is. But I have a feeling you are capable of doing it. I have heard you sing, after all."

"But only from a distance."

"It makes no difference. I heard enough to be able to judge."

"What do *you* know about it?" Her voice held scorn.

His eyes flickered for a moment and his grandfather moved as if to speak, but changed his mind. Carina rose and walked across to confront her tormentor, every inch of her body prepared to do battle.

"I'll agree to sing, Mr. de Verrier, if you're really interested," she sounded doubtful, "but *with* my guitar, not without it."

He did not move. The guitar was still firmly in his hold. With a movement born of desperation, she tried to unfasten his fingers from the instrument, but she might as well have tried to wrench out the roots of an ancient tree.

He smiled at her futile attempts to free her "treasure" and moved a hand to take hold of her left one, turning it palm upwards and rubbing his thumb over the hard skin which had formed on her fingertips.

"As I thought," he murmured, "the hallmark of the dedicated – and addicted – guitar player."

"All right," she conceded a little sulkily, "so it's a habit with me. I love my guitar, in fact I can't do without it."

"She's obstinate, boy," Ernest said, "dead obstinate. Go on – let her have it back."

Marcus relented and she took the guitar in her arms like a mother cradling a baby. She left him as if she were trying to escape arrest, and he smiled mockingly at her speedy retreat.

"Now sing, Carrie," Ernest urged again.

13

She sat on the footstool and strummed the instrument, bending her head and listening lovingly to the sound it made. She paused, took a breath, let it go and said, "I can't."

"Why not?" The question came sharply from the younger man.

"It's no use. I can't sing in an unsympathetic atmosphere."

Ernest eased himself agitatedly to the front of the armchair. "But, Carrie, I'm not unsympathetic, you know that."

She answered helplessly, "It's not you, Mr. de Verrier. It's your grandson."

"Him, *unsympathetic*, Carrie? But he's a musician, a professional musician. Didn't you guess? He's a pianist, but not only that, he's a music teacher."

"A teacher of *singing*, Miss Ascott, amongst other things." The words were spoken softly but, in retaliation for her accusation of lack of sympathy, with the faintest spicing of malice.

Her eyes opened wide. "But that makes it worse. I definitely can't sing now. You'd be too critical."

"I promise not to be too critical," he said, as if humouring a child. "Now will you sing for me?"

She closed her eyes, shutting him out. "I'll sing for your grandfather." She opened them, alarmed. "I'm sorry," to Marcus, "I didn't mean to be rude. But, you see, I always sing for your grandfather, whenever he's there."

"Which I usually am, lass, aren't I?" He shifted back in the chair. "Needs support, that girl. Always needs bolstering up. Never known a girl so uncertain of herself."

Now his grandson's eyes opened wide. He looked her over cynically and incredulously. This girl, he seemed to be thinking, uncertain of herself, with the wealth which surely must be present in the very air she breathes?

But all he said was, his voice curt, "What will you sing, Miss Ascott?"

14

"I'll sing," she said, "the sort of song so many young people sing these days and," she looked at him quickly and looked away, "the sort of song you no doubt will uncompromisingly condemn. And despise. Because you simply won't understand it."

"Meaning, I suppose, I'm too old?"

"No, too prejudiced." Her eyes met his levelly. "Your academic background sticks out a mile, and academics are always intellectual snobs."

Ernest laughed, but Marcus flushed with anger. "So you've classified me, have you, Miss Ascott? Labelled me and filed me away as being bigoted, ignorant and intolerant towards anything outside my own field? Isn't it a little early in our acquaintance to do that?"

"You've labelled *me*, Mr. de Verrier," she answered calmly. "I can see it in your eyes."

"She bites, lad," Ernest said, "when she's provoked. You'll learn."

"Try me, Miss Ascott. Academic or not, as a musician – and a teacher – I have been trained to be impartial."

There was a long pause while she channelled her thoughts into the right mood. "Your grandfather has heard this song before. I wrote the words. Seth wrote the music."

"Seth? Your fiancé?"

"Fiancé? I haven't got a fiancé. I'm not engaged." She rubbed the back of the hand with the ring on it against her side with a quick, unconscious gesture, as if trying to rub the ring away. "Seth is a friend. He's a member of our music group. We all write songs, our sort of songs, both the music and the lyrics."

"Of the kind you're about to sing?"

She nodded, closed her eyes again, played a few introductory bars and said over the sound, "It's called *Think of a life.*"

She sang, her voice low, rising now and then to a husky sweetness,

Think of a life
*   Without pain or sorrow,*
Think of a day
*   With a peaceful tomorrow.*
Think of a world
*   Without rich, without poor,*
Where what's to come hurts less than before.

Think of a life
*   Without fighting or strife,*
Think of a world where peace is,
*   Think of a day*
When fear's gone away
*   And the whole of mankind*
Comes together to say,
*   We'll end all the hatred*
And let love have its way."

The silence was deep and broken only after long moments by a gruff, "Thanks, lass." There was no comment from the grandson.

Disappointed, Carina put aside her guitar and went into the kitchen to make the promised cup of tea.

She put on the kettle, found a tray and placed three cups and saucers on it. She knew her way about Ernest's kitchen better than her own. Her skin prickled again and she swung round to find herself being watched. She wished the man would not creep up on her like that.

"You know how to make tea, Miss Ascott?" The sarcasm was there and she bridled, flinging it back at him.

"It's a simple enough operation, Mr. de Verrier. So simple that even someone with a low intelligence quotient could do it." She smiled at him sweetly. "So perhaps I could teach you some time?"

He smiled back. "No need, I already know. But it explains how even you could learn to do it." She swung away from him. He had won that point.

He sat sideways on a chair, hooking his arm over the back. "Isn't the song you have just sung what is usually called a 'protest' song?"

"Yes." She frowned, on the defensive at once. "I knew you wouldn't understand it or like it. I warned you."

"On the contrary, I echo every single sentiment expressed in it. Congratulations."

She eyed him doubtfully. "Are you being honest?"

"Perfectly." He smiled. "Sorry to deprive you of the opposition you so obviously wanted, and which young people nowadays seem to thrive on."

"And my – singing?" She poured the tea into the cups, trying to look unconcerned.

He laughed now, really laughed, his eyes lighting up. "So you want my opinion! After all you've said!" He looked at her reflectively, as if sensing for himself the uncertainty to which his grandfather had referred. "No comment, except to say," he paused, choosing his words, "it was pleasant to listen to."

Carina nodded, evidently satisfied and expecting no more. He watched her, narrowing his eyes as if profoundly mystified by her apparent modesty. She lifted the tray, but he rose swiftly and took it from her, carrying it through the hall into the living-room. Ernest, who was dozing, came awake at the rattle of cups and took his tea, expressing his gratitude. Carina drank hers, put the cup aside and picked up her guitar.

She looked at Marcus, the frown in place again. "You wouldn't be interested –? No, of course you wouldn't. With your scholarly background you couldn't be expected to –"

"To what?"

"I was just wondering," she stopped, still uncertain as to whether she should be asking such a man such a question, "whether you would like to come along to our music group. But," she added quickly, "I know you wouldn't like it, so forget it." She turned her attention to her guitar.

"Do you make a habit," came the dry voice, "in the

17

rarefied social atmosphere in which you must surely live," the words were a feeler and he waited for a denial, but none came, "to issue an invitation, only to withdraw it the moment after it's given?"

Carina coloured, her eyes as well as her fingers moving over the guitar strings. "I'm sorry. It's just that I didn't want to embarrass you."

"I'm not the sensitive plant you seem to think I am, Miss Ascott." His voice had hardened. "Circumstances – past experiences – have toughened me up considerably."

She wondered what he meant by that. A broken relationship with a woman? An unhappy marriage, perhaps? Although for some inexplicable reason her mind recoiled from the thought of his being a married man.

"Well, then," she still did not look at him, "would you join us? We meet every Saturday afternoon, come rain or shine, in a prearranged place, go for a walk in the forest, have tea in a café, and walk back. Then we all collect at my house and play our instruments and sing."

"Don't your parents object to the noise you make? Or are they long-suffering?"

"My father had a building put up in our gr –" She had nearly said "grounds", but checked herself, changing the word with a certain amount of inaccuracy to "garden" because it sounded more modest. She had already guessed that the younger de Verrier was no worshipper of either affluence or influence. "He had it sound-proofed – to spare the neighbours' feelings – and we play and sing in there."

"Tell me the time and place of meeting," he had his diary out, "and I'll be there."

While Carina washed up, the sound of her guitar came through to the kitchen. It was being played experimentally, and she almost dropped the saucer she was holding when she heard an extract from the song she and Seth had composed being picked out with unbelievable accuracy.

She ran to the door of the living-room and stared. Marcus smiled crookedly. "How am I doing, Miss Ascott?

18

Do I pass your rigid test? Do I qualify to become a member of your very select group, despite my thirty or so years?"

"It's great!" she exclaimed. "To remember it so accurately after only hearing it once . . ."

He bowed mockingly.

"I told you, Carrie," Ernest could not keep the pride from his voice, "he's an expert, a professional."

Marcus handed over the guitar. "You see, I haven't harmed it."

She said, a little shyly, "I didn't really think you would."

Ernest de Verrier chuckled, "Looks like you've gained her trust already, Marcus."

"If not her liking?" Marcus's eyes were challenging.

"I've hardly known you long enough, have I, to decide one way or the other?"

"I thought women knew instantly whether they liked a man or not."

"Oh no." She took him seriously. "Some quite horrible men, when you get to know them, can turn out to be very pleasant people."

He laughed loudly. "Then there's hope for me."

"Oh," she considered him, "I wouldn't call you horrible. Just — just," she sought for a word, "difficult."

Ernest, standing by his grandson, nudged him. "She's got tact, Marcus, that you can't deny."

As the two men stood side by side, the one tall and vigorous, the other bent with age, Carina, whose habit it was to search for family likenesses, could see that Ernest de Verrier must once have been as handsome and commanding as his grandson. But she doubted whether he had also possessed the younger man's autocratic manner.

Marcus went to the door. "I won't trouble you with my 'difficult' presence any longer, Miss Ascott." He turned and asked, "I take it you won't be requiring a lift home?"

"No, thanks. My car's outside."

19

"That slinky white sports model I saw you arrive in? Is it yours or your father's?"

"Mine." Her tone was almost apologetic.

His eyes narrowed critically as he looked her over. "Yes, I thought it might be." He sprinted up the stairs as if he could not get away from her fast enough.

Ernest insisted on going with Carina to her car. He put on his coat because, he said, although it was still August, he was sure he could feel an autumn chill in the air.

"Mr. de Verrier, is your grandson married?"

"Married? No, my dear. Doubt if he ever will now. He's married to his music. It's his life. He lives and breathes it." They stood at the kerb. "He was engaged a few years ago. The girl was a beauty, a musician like himself. He fell for her really hard, asked her to marry him and she said yes. He spent most of his savings on an engagement ring, and even then I don't think she considered it good enough for her. I told him he was mad – she was outside his world. He'd never be able to keep up with her, he'd never earn enough. Her parents had money, and not only that. They were members of the aristocracy, had some sort of fancy title. They didn't approve of him, thought their daughter was marrying beneath her. So they talked her out of it."

"What happened?"

"Just before the wedding the girl broke off the engagement and promptly got herself engaged and married to someone else – son of an earl."

"I expect that pleased her parents."

"You're too right, Carrie, but it broke Marcus's heart. Never again, he said. It was no women for him from then on, especially 'expensive' ones, as he called it."

"So it's no girl-friends either?"

"Oh, he has a lady-friend now and then, but nothing fancy, if you know what I mean. Quiet girls – 'insipid' I think is the word – nothing in them, not much character. And not much money, either!" He laughed. "He's on his guard now. In a way I can't blame him, but –" He lifted his

20

shoulders. "Seems a pity if he lets one stupid girl put him off women for good and all."

"So he's filled his life with music?"

"To the brim, my dear, to the very brim."

She waited until Ernest had gone back into the house and drove herself home.

The Ascott residence was a blaze of lights as Carina approached. The Ascotts never felt the need to economise on electricity – or anything else. Carina swept into the semicircular drive and braked in the car port in front of the double garage. They were a four-car family and when Justine, her younger sister, was home, Carina's car was invariably the one to be pushed out to stand all the time in the open air.

Carina trod the stone steps to the front door. The house had been built in the early part of the century and had been extensively modernised both inside and out by the present owners. But the regal pillars which had been built into the entrance porch had been allowed to remain. Whether they were intended to impress or intimidate, Carina had never decided.

But since most visitors to the house were usually required to be of an exceptional quality and status – it was a wonder, Carina often thought, that they were not first made to pass a means test! – she came to the conclusion that the pillars had been permitted to stay there as an indication of what was to come, as part of the build-up to the refined and exclusive atmosphere inside.

The entrance hall played a similar role. It was richly carpeted and furnished as if it were the lounge-foyer of an expensive hotel. To Carina, the house was not a home. It was too artificial and pretentious.

Although Carina had lived there since childhood, she had never developed a sense of belonging to the place. She knew instinctively that she did not fit in. Nor did she fit in with her parents' ideas of how a daughter of theirs should

21

behave, whether adopted, as Carina was, or by birth, like Justine.

Long ago they had called Carina their "little rebel", saying that as she grew older she would lose her "rebellious" ways and conform to the behaviour pattern expected of a girl with parents of their financial and social standing.

But it had not happened, and they no longer talked of their "little rebel" with indulgent affection, but instead with irritation and a resigned shrug of the shoulders. "What could they do with her?" they asked themselves. She was not of their flesh, as Justine was.

Phyllis Ascott came down the stairs, eyeing her daughter as if she were an Alsatian dog of uncertain temper. Would she snap or would she nuzzle? Since Carina had never been known to ingratiate herself with anyone, Phyllis appeared to decide that it would be advisable to humour her. She smiled, but as a greeting it was restrained. Carina was familiar with that smile. She had seen it so often, placed on her mother's face as a duty to the attractive yet unrelentingly recalcitrant daughter Phyllis and her husband Lloyd had taken unto their barren selves eighteen years before.

Phyllis said, "Where have you been, dear? With the old man again?"

"Yes. I sang to the old people, then I took him home."

Her mother murmured a vague "Oh", and glanced at her watch. "You're later than usual. We began to worry."

"I'm sorry. I should have rung. I didn't realise you would worry about me."

"We always worry about you."

That, Carina knew, was intended to convey to her what a burden her unpredictable, unorthodox ways were to them.

Carina began to climb the stairs. "I met Mr. de Verrier's grandson."

"Did you, dear?" The response held the barest trace of interest.

"He's a musician. He's living there now."

· But her mother had not bothered to listen. She was on her way to tell her husband that Carina was back at last, back from visiting that awful old man she was so friendly with.

For ten years the Ascotts had patiently awaited the arrival of their firstborn. They had been reassured at regular intervals by their doctor that there was no physical reason why they should not conceive a child. But, despite these repeated assurances, they finally gave up hope. When a tragic accident orphaned the little daughter of an acquaintance of theirs, they opened their hearts to the black-haired, wide-eyed four-year-old called Carina Adams and took her into their home.

In due course they adopted her and she became Carina Ascott. Less than two years later a child of their own, Justine, was on her way. When she was born, fair, with delicate features, resembling her mother in so many ways, the new baby became their pride and delight — and their whole world.

It could not be denied that Phyllis and Lloyd still loved Carina. After all, they said to her and to each other, she was theirs by choice. But it did not take long for the sensitive six-year-old to realise that she now came second in their lives. It was the beginning of Carina's rebelliousness, not of flagrant opposition, but more of a doggedly persistent refusal to conform, to do what was expected of her.

Carina placed her guitar on the armchair. Her bedroom had been fitted out as a bed-sitter by her parents, who were ready to lavish any amount of money on her to keep her happy. Was their benevolence, Carina often wondered, merely a salve to their consciences, because they could not give her the love they gave their real daughter? Then she would chide herself for such thoughts, because her parents had given her so much.

She threw herself on to the bed, crumpling the chunky, down-filled quilt, and closed her eyes. She could still remember with horrifying clarity the terrible accident which

23

had deprived her of her real parents and grandparents at one blow.

They were on the motorway driving north for a fortnight's holiday. The car had been a four-seater, so Carina had been sitting on her grandmother's knee in the back. An articulated lorry on the other carriageway had careered out of control across the central reservation, slicing into their car, throwing the child clear, but bringing her world, as she knew it, to a tragic end. She had been three years old.

Her other grandparents had been far away in New Zealand and were, in any case, in uncertain health. So she had been placed in a children's home. She could still remember the day when, nearly a year later, a man and a woman had come to see her, telling her they had known her "mummy and daddy", and were going to take her home with them. Then they would look after her for "ever and ever".

Carina had gone with them willingly enough, thinking that they were taking her to her real mother and father. But when they had asked her to call them "Mummy and Daddy", she had known the truth, and had cried for hours, and they hadn't known why.

When, about eighteen months later, they had told her she was going to have "a little brother or sister", she had been delighted. But when the little sister was born, and she saw her adoptive parents' love branch away from her like a train leaving one track for another, she felt herself shunted into an emotional siding, and her world had gone crashing about her ears once more.

Now she thought of Ernest de Verrier and of how much he had come to mean to her. He had taken the place of the grandparents she had lost. She did have grandparents, of course – her adoptive ones – who were kindness itself. But she felt that whenever they came to the house they were watching her for any doubtful inherited characteristics, not of their making, and which could not be laid at their door.

There were times when she longed to forget she was

adopted. It was like a terrible pain, a wound that would not heal. Sometimes she wished her adoptive parents were poor instead of rich – then she could have better identified with them.

She had told Ernest her story, her feelings and her deepest longings, and had sworn him to secrecy. She had told no one else. She felt she could trust him never to divulge her secret come what may, and knew his grandson would never come to hear of it through Ernest's lips.

She thought of Marcus de Verrier and found herself hoping that he would keep his promise to meet them at the weekend. Remembering the remoteness of his manner, his disdain for all he thought she represented, she had no hope at all that he would come.

A letter was propped against her dressing-table mirror. It bore a Brazilian postmark and she guessed it was from Avery. He was an employee of her father's, an executive although only twenty-five and, because of his social connections, had been pushed to a level of authority unmerited by his ability. He had public school and Oxford University behind him, plus family wealth almost, but not quite, equal to that of the Ascotts.

He was considered by Phyllis and Lloyd as being eminently suitable as a future husband for their elder daughter. As far as they were concerned, the sooner her marriage to him could take place, the sooner she and her awkwardness would be taken off their hands. But as was to be expected, Carina herself was proving an almost insurmountable barrier to their plans.

Before Avery Brand had left for South America he had proposed to Carina. She had refused, but Avery had been warned that she might be "difficult" about it. It had not deterred him because the thought of being united to a family with even more wealth at its disposal than his own had spurred him on to try his luck. And Carina, with her dark beauty, her defensive yet challenging eyes, her shapeliness and her fight – there was no other word for it – attrac-

25

ted him more than any other girl of his acquaintance.

The night before he had left for South America he had taken the solitaire diamond ring from his pocket. He had lifted her left hand and tried to push the ring on to her third finger, but she had obstinately refused to allow him to do so. His determination, however, increased with her refusal, which he thought anyway she might be putting on to make herself more desirable, but she had won. He had, however, managed to reach a compromise with her.

"Now I've bought it," he had said, "at least wear it, Carina – on your right hand, if not your left. I'll be away six months. By then you'll be so delighted to see me, you'll fall into my arms!" She had shaken her head, but he had persisted, "Then we'll make our engagement official."

She opened his letter, reading with some scepticism the declaration of love he had never actually spoken. She read with greater interest his description of the country in which he was staying and of how he was coping with the language problem and spending his evenings studying phrase books and learning essential words. He was also enjoying himself, he added, although not half as much as if she were with him.

She threw the letter down in disgust. She was as outside Avery's world as Marcus de Verrier had been outside the world of his one-time fiancée's.

Which brought her back to Marcus de Verrier. She wondered where he was working, whether his "new job" had any connection with music – but it must have, since he described himself as a music teacher. She picked up her guitar and, late though it was, she picked out the melody of the song she and Seth had written, and which Marcus had remembered and played after she had sung it to him.

The music brought his face into focus before her eyes with disturbing clarity, so she stopped playing because that seemed to be the only way to get the man out of her mind.

26

CHAPTER TWO

MARCUS kept his promise after all, and joined them on their walk. Carina stood with the others and as his car drew up, her heart lifted in a way which alarmed her. They were gathered on the edge of the forest, across the road from Ascott House, and they listened with interest as Carina told them who the stranger was.

As Marcus emerged from his car, and his age became apparent – he could easily have given many of them ten years or more – their interest became merely polite and a little distant as they wondered what could have possessed Carina to invite him. He would pour cold water on the whole afternoon, no doubt about that. He was old, they were thinking, he must be at least thirty.

But as Carina looked at him, he appeared to her to have lost four or five years since she had last seen him. He was smiling, he was approachable, and he was dressed in clothes almost as casual as those of her friends. But he had done it cleverly. He had gone so far and no farther, enough to lower the barriers of age and outlook, but not so far as to merit any accusation of "dressing down" to his companions and trying to meet them entirely on their own level.

As Carina introduced them, they treated Marcus with respect, and also with reserve. "This," Carina said, "is Mr. –"

"Marcus," he prompted.

"Marcus de Verrier. M—Marcus," she stumbled over his name, "Marcus, this is Seth." Seth nodded. "Dave, Sandra, Olwen," she went round the group.

They waited for a few minutes for possible latecomers and Marcus said, "Carina?"

Startled at hearing him speak her name, she turned.

He raised his hand and pointed. "Your home?" Since "Ascott House" was carved in the stonework around the front door, each letter with its own flourish, he must have known the answer to the question before he asked it.

"Of course," she said carelessly, trying by her tone of voice to minimise the importance of the fact.

By his expression, she could see he had misinterpreted her offhand response, taking it to have a very different meaning from that intended. To him it had obviously implied that she regarded the grandeur of the place she lived in as nothing unusual, and was so inured to the luxuries such a residence must contain that she took them for granted.

"I was surprised you bothered to come," she said to him as they moved off through the forest. Since he knew no one else, she was obliged to walk with him. The trees were in full leaf, without even a hint of bronze about their greenness to warn of the coming of autumn.

"Were you?" He smiled askance at her. "Then it shows how little you know about me. I always keep my promises, unlike some – women I know."

She supposed he was referring to his broken romance. She said indignantly, "*I* keep my promises, too."

"Do you?" He was plainly sceptical. "I have discovered, through bitter experience, that the greater the wealth and social standing of an individual, the greater the ease with which he – or she – breaks a promise."

"Who's talking about wealth?" Seth had dropped behind the others and joined them. The group in front slowed down.

"If you want to know about wealth," said Dave, "ask Carina."

28

"You've heard of living below the poverty line, Marcus," said a bearded young man called Luke, "well, Carina knows all about the opposite – how to live above the prosperity line."

"It's not true," Carina protested, her voice rising, "you're giving Marcus the wrong impression."

But they pursued their prey relentlessly. "Carina's our 'Exhibit A'," Sandra joined in, "the wealthy one amongst us poverty-stricken types."

"Poor little rich girl," said Seth.

"Seth, how *could* you?"

He heard the tears in her voice and put his arm across her shoulders. Marcus glanced at her, puzzled by her tone and the defenceless look on her face.

"The perpetual student," Dave commented. "Has she told you, Marcus –"

"I haven't told him anything," Carina snapped. "How could I, when I only met him three days ago and then for about an hour?"

Dave persisted, "Has she told you how she's done no work since leaving school?"

"You're wrong, Dave. I took a course in shorthand and typing."

"And gave it up because it bored you."

"It didn't bore me. It was because –" How could she tell them she had been so bad at it compared with all the others, she couldn't bear being left so far behind?

"Then," Dave went on, "she had a go at art."

"And did that suit you, Carina?" The cynical note in Marcus's voice told her that he was accepting unquestioningly all they were saying about her – in order, no doubt, to hold it against her at some future time.

"No, it did not," she snapped. "It was my father's idea –"

"By then," Olwen commented, "he'd got so fed up with having you hanging round the house that if you'd suggested taking a course in walking on the moon's surface, he would

29

have agreed!"

Carina was bewildered. Why were they ganging up on her like this?

"So you discovered you were no artist, Carina?" It was Marcus, again, probing, sarcastic.

"I couldn't even grasp the basic principles," she muttered. And, she thought but did not add, I had no confidence in myself and there was no one to encourage me and tell me I could do it if I tried. "So," she said aloud, "I gave it up."

"There's only one thing left for you to do, Carina," Seth said, his arm still round her. "Get married."

"To you?" asked Marcus, watching them.

"To *me*? You must be joking! Carina's so used to the luxuries of life, she'll have to marry a millionaire to keep up with her expensive tastes."

What was the matter with them all today? she thought despairingly. Why was she the butt of all their jokes? Were they showing off in front of Marcus? Or was this what they really thought of her, deep down, and now it was all coming out? She grew frightened, seeing the one real happiness she cherished – the company of these ordinary, simple-living, unaffected young people – being torn from her grasp like the last remaining piece of shelter in a tornado.

"She's engaged, anyway," Sandra said enviously, "to a wealthy young man employed by her father. Haven't you seen her ring?"

"I'm *not* engaged!" She turned on Sandra. "I'm *not*! Here, you can have the darned thing, I don't want it." She tore the ring from her finger and held it out to the girl.

They all laughed and her lips trembled. She turned her face against Seth's chest and he held her there for a few moments. He motioned the others away. "Sorry, Carina. We didn't mean it, you know."

Marcus bent down to pick up the diamond ring which had slipped unheeded from her fingers. "Carina, your ring."

30

She pulled herself together, wiped her eyes and turned to him. She held out her hand, but instead of giving it to her, he slipped it on to her finger – her engagement finger.

He watched her for a few moments, as if testing her. Suddenly it came to her what he had done. She gazed up at him, her eyes wide and puzzled, then she muttered, "Wrong finger. I told you, I'm not engaged," and moved it to her right hand.

"What will you do now, Carina?" Marcus asked, as Seth walked ahead.

"Try something else."

There was a long silence. The walkers moved in an uneven line through the forest, taking the well-worn paths, negotiating the roots of trees, avoiding the straggling blackberry bushes, and brushing the bracken with their legs. There was birdsong above and around them and their feet trailed in the trodden-down leaves of past summers.

"How did it come about," Marcus asked after a while, "that you started this pastime of singing to old people?"

"It was a collective idea. We decided to visit clubs and old people's homes. It seems to work."

"But don't you find it difficult to communicate with people so much older than yourselves?"

"It's not as difficult as you think," she said defensively, "for young people to make emotional contact with the old. Sometimes I explain the meaning of the song I'm going to sing, as if it were in a foreign language – which perhaps it is to them – so that they can follow it better when I'm actually singing it."

"And what's your aim in doing all this?"

"To help older people to grow more tolerant of youth, perhaps by reminding them of what it was like for them when they were young. I love singing to old people. They're so ready to give you their sympathy and encouragement."

"It all sounds very laudable," he still seemed unconvinced by her explanation, "but if they wanted to sing their songs to *you*, would you listen with the sympathy you expect from them when you're singing your songs?"

"I go further than that," she said triumphantly, "I sing *their* songs to *them*, songs of their younger days. Ask your grandfather. But I also give them, through my songs, a vision of the future as it could be if we all really tried. When I sing to them of youth's struggles for a better world now, they remember their struggles to achieve the same things when they were young."

"What," he asked, laughing without humour and bringing the conversation back to a personal level, "do *you* know about struggles? You, with your cushioned background?"

She answered quietly, "I know more about — struggles and difficulties than you think."

"Yes," he said cynically, "difficulties of your own making. Look at the way you're drifting aimlessly through life. Who else has imposed that on you but yourself? That and perhaps your too secure way of life."

"And what," she snapped back, "do you know of my way of life?"

There was mockery in his answering smile. "I have eyes in my head. One has only to look at you and hear you speak to guess at the ease and comfort in which you must live. You may not know it, but — to me, at any rate — you're an open book. I'm speaking from experience. I've known your type before. To my cost."

Her brown eyes rebuked him. "Doesn't it occur to you that you may be under an illusion about me? That you might be only half right? Isn't it advisable sometimes to read between the lines, even in a book? Mightn't there sometimes be something more there which the writer hasn't actually written but only implied?"

He raised an eyebrow. "Exactly what are you trying to do? Chase after my good opinion and get me to pay homage to you as my grandfather does? And thus procure yet another de Verrier scalp for your belt?"

She flushed deeply at his derisive tone, and answered

32

indignantly, "Of course not. I'm simply trying to tell you that if you are 'reading' me, as you imply, then you're doing so with your eyes shut."

"Thanks for the compliment to my discriminatory powers. But I know enough about you to form an opinion of you."

"Which isn't very flattering?"

He did not reply.

"Well," she said, forcing her tone to be offhanded, "your grandfather likes me and that, as far as I'm concerned, is all that matters. Whether you like me or not is immaterial to me." But she knew with a stab of fear that it was not.

They had sandwiches and scones and home-made cakes at a café on the edge of the forest. Marcus insisted on paying for everyone.

"We have another plutocrat among us," Luke laughed, "another one in Carina's class."

"Let me assure you," Marcus said, his eyes glinting at the girl in question, "that neither financially nor socially am I in Carina's class. My way of life and hers are a world apart." He looked at her challengingly. "And I shall do my utmost to keep it that way."

The others applauded, but Carina countered feelingly, "What I can't understand is how an intelligent man like you can let prejudice and past experience warp your judgment so disastrously."

"You're wrong. My judgment is not warped. I'm simply looking at life through plain glass these days, instead of the tinted spectacles I wore in my innocent youth."

"Aren't you carrying your disenchantment a bit too far? What you're really doing is transferring the grudge you bear against one human being quite indiscriminately to another. Even if I concede that your judgment isn't warped — which I don't — you must admit that you're being very unfair."

What was she doing, arguing with him like this? Pleading her own case? To what end, and with what particular

33

purpose in mind? She hardly knew the man. Why should she solicit his good opinion as though it meant more than anything in the world to her?

He looked at her lingeringly, as though he was guessing her thoughts. He closed the argument. "Unfortunately for you, I am one of those people – admittedly rare – who learns and profits by experience."

He paid for the tea, warning them that next time it would be back to normal and every man – and woman – for himself.

So, Carina thought, with a flick of pleasure, he's intending to come again?

They took another route home. The others drifted ahead, leaving Carina and Marcus together.

"Have you any brothers and sisters?" Marcus asked.

"A sister, Justine, five years younger than I am. She's seventeen."

"Which makes you twenty-two. Does she live at home?"

"Usually, but at the moment she's on a Mediterranean cruise. Then she's going to a finishing school in Switzerland."

"And," with a tight, sardonic smile, "were you also – finished?"

"They tried, but I'm afraid they didn't even 'begin'. I didn't give them the chance. It was the same at boarding school."

She could not tell him how the school, with its regulated, closed-in atmosphere, had reminded her of the children's home in which she had stayed after her parents' deaths; or of how she had felt just as abandoned there and deprived of love as after that terrible accident. Nor could she confide in him how profoundly shocked she had been when she had overheard her parents debating one day whether or not to send Justine to boarding school. They had decided that she was too precious to them to be sent away, implying to the sensitive child who had accidentally overheard their discussion that she was not.

"So," Marcus said with a faint smile, "you resisted the treatment from start to finish, the pressure to conform, to acquire socially acceptable manners and," he eyed her briefly, "dress?"

"With all my being," she answered fiercely.

"All the same," he said with a touch of scorn, "I'm sorry to tell you that the breeding shows. There's a certain — superior air about you. As I said, I've come across it before, at close quarters. The impeccable upper class manner, the result of years of indoctrination by the staff of exclusive fee-paying educational establishments for daughters of the privileged classes. Whether you like it or not, you have acquired it."

"I don't believe you," she said evenly, meeting his mocking eyes. "You're seeing that 'superior air' in me because you want to. You're looking at me with eyes so prejudiced you can't see me as I really am."

"I notice that you're pleading your case again." The quizzical eyebrow rose. "I wonder why?" She bit her lip angrily. "But," he went on, "whether you're right or not about my attitude, there's one thing I'm certain about — I'm not getting my fingers burnt again."

There was a brief, charged silence as the warning — surely that was what he had intended it to be? — hung in the air. Then he asked, "Tell me, did your parents get the message about your resisting the 'treatment'?"

"Yes. In the end they took me away from finishing school. Then they gave me up." She sighed. "They don't like my friends, they don't like my guitar, they don't like the way I go round singing to people. They don't like —" She caught her breath, glancing up at him with a quick, frightened look.

But he had guessed. "Your friendship with my grandfather?" She nodded. "I thought as much." There was a short silence. "You know, it puzzles me, this fondness of yours for him."

She could not tell him, "Your grandfather's the anchor
35

in my world, the one stable factor in my life, the only person to whom I've told my story and to whom I feel I can run whenever I need reassurance."

He was waiting for an answer, so she compromised with, "He's a very nice man. I —" Should she say it? "I look on him as *my* grandfather." She glanced up at him shyly. "I hope you don't mind?"

He laughed. "Not in the least. He has granddaughters of his own, of course, but they're not at all like you. More —" he considered her, "more sophisticated, as I would have imagined someone with your background would be." There was a question in the silence, but she did not answer it. "Surely you have grandparents yourself?"

After the barest hesitation, she nodded. He was waiting for more, but she did not satisfy his curiosity. They were nearly home, and Carina was glad. She did not know how long she could have continued to parry his questions.

Carina always took her friends to the "den", as they called it, through the side entrance into the gardens of her home. The house itself was a large and imposing construction, the main part having been added to on both sides, giving it over all a rather rambling appearance.

Even from the back it looked impressive. With a sinking heart, Carina caught Marcus's look, which was shot through with contempt as he surveyed the Ascott home. His eyes swept round the ornate grounds, taking in the velvety lawns, the lily pond, the flower beds and rose gardens, all of which spoke plainly of the loving attention they received from the band of gardeners employed to tend them.

Anger stirred inside her for his scornful attitude and as the others trooped into the large brick-built den, she said to him, "There's no need to show your dislike of where I live quite so openly."

"*Dislike* it, Carina?" There was ingenuous astonishment in his voice. "Who could possibly dislike such a beautiful house? Wealth oozes from it to such an extent that it's a wonder money isn't spilling out of the doors and windows."

"You," she said between her teeth, "are nothing more than a supercilious, *inverted* snob!"

He countered, his eyes laughing at her, "Forgive me if I'm wrong, but isn't that a contradiction in terms? After all, I can hardly be both supercilious *and* an inverted snob, can I?"

She gave him a scathing look and swept into the den, annoyed because he was not annoyed. She told herself defiantly – and quite untruthfully – that she did not care whether he followed her or not. He wandered in behind her, however, and sat in one of the fireside chairs with which the place was furnished. It was so well decorated and fitted out that many families would have cheerfully lived in it permanently. There was even a tiny kitchen, where tea or coffee could be brewed and a light meal cooked.

Carina glanced at Marcus, as if daring him to comment on the luxuriously appointed building which she had so casually referred to as her "den", but he merely smiled at her, a smile as untinted and over-sweet as white icing on a cake.

Carina reached for her guitar. The others were already tuning theirs. Marcus's eyes were caught by an object across the room. He walked over to it. "A harpsichord, Carina?" He fingered the keys without actually sounding them. "How come?"

Seth joined him. "We use it as background for our playing. It makes a fabulous sound, giving the tunes a – a sort of richness, for want of a better word."

"It's an antique," Marcus commented, his eyebrows high. "I suppose you appreciate that, Carina?"

"Of course. My father gave it to me. I said I'd like a harpsichord, so he told me to look for one. I searched the antique shops and found this."

"So he bought it, just like that? Money no object?"

There he was, rubbing it in again.

"The power of money, Marcus!" Seth said, laughing. "It can buy everything, didn't you know?"

"Can it?" Marcus murmured, looking at Carina, who coloured fiercely and returned to her seat. 'It can't buy me,' his look had said.

Marcus asked, "May I?" and sat himself on the stool in front of the harpsichord. He played it with the ease of an expert and his listeners stared. After a while he stopped and said, "Sorry about the classical stuff. That's more my line than yours."

"It was great," they said, accepting him more and more as the moments passed.

"Can you play it, Carina?" Marcus asked, and when she nodded, lifted his eyebrows in surprise. "Let me hear you."

There was a quiet but authoritative note in his voice which made her respond automatically to his command. She sat on the stool and played the ancient instrument with commendable skill. When she had finished he nodded, but to her disappointment made no comment, asking instead, "You play the piano?"

"Yes but I prefer the guitar. Come on," to the others, "let's sing. That's what we're here for."

Each sang and played in turn, with Carina holding back until Marcus, who had been listening with deep interest to each performance said, "Carina? Your turn now."

There was the authority again, but although she found herself wanting to rebel, she obeyed. "I'll sing Seth's and my song, *Think of a life*. Seth, you play, I'll sing."

She did not put her guitar away from her, but held it on her lap, and as she sang, her fingers idly stroked the strings, as if in her mind she was accompanying herself. She did not watch Marcus as she sang. She closed her eyes and imagined it was his grandfather who was listening to her, with his loving approval and understanding.

There was a short silence at the end of her song – the strange, taut silence to which she had grown accustomed, because it greeted the end of each one of her performances, no matter where she sang.

"Carina?" She opened her eyes and stared at Marcus,

trying to clear her vision. For a fleeting moment she had imagined it was his grandfather sitting there. Was there so much of the older man in the younger that one day Marcus might come to mean as much to her as his grandfather did?

The thought made her shrink into herself, and when Marcus held out his hand, indicating that he wanted her guitar, she clasped it to her as though she were prepared to sacrifice her life rather than give it to him.

"Carina, you sing, I'll play." The others watched the battle of wills with fascinated interest.

"No," she glared at him, "I'll sing, I'll play."

He leaned forward. "You know *Plaisir d'Amour*?" She nodded. "In French? Right. Give me your guitar."

Their eyes met and his contained the command she seemed unable to withstand. His whole personality emitted a magnetism which she found both irresistible and frightening, and she found herself handing over her instrument as though he possessed the power to take from her whatever he wanted.

There was a brief but unmistakable glint of triumph in his eyes. He moved to sit on one of the high stools, lifted a foot, placing it on a metal bar near the base of the stool and rested the guitar on his knee. He tuned it with the touch of an expert, played the first few bars of the song experimentally, and nodded to Carina that he was ready for her to begin.

He played the introduction again, and waited. She could not start. Her guitar had been taken from her. She shook her head. He said, with infinite patience, "Clasp your hands, tight as you like, but you are not getting this guitar back *until you have sung.*"

She clasped her hands as he had told her, so tightly that it hurt, and began to sing. Because of her tension, her voice was tight and strained, but as her ears picked up the beauty of his playing, she lost her nervousness and matched her performance to his. She realised how sensitively he was accompanying her and how he was listening to her as well as to the sound he was making. His mind seemed to be reaching out to her, urging her on. She made contact with his urgency and absorbed it into her own mind and singer and player became as one.

There was that breath-holding silence at the end, then came a burst of applause which she had never heard before from her companions.

"That's great," Seth cried. "You two should go around together. You should team up. You were made for each other — strictly in the musical sense, of course," he added with a grin.

"Good thing you qualified that statement, Seth," Marcus commented. "For one awful moment I thought you were trying to marry us off to each other."

Carina rose, the colour high in her cheeks, and took the guitar from him. He smiled. "I knew you could sing without it."

"I hated it. You had no right to take it from me."

"I agree. No right at all. Call it, if you like, an experiment."

She turned away, then turned back. She hated herself for asking it, but asked nevertheless, "How did I sing?"

He laughed, as if amused by her seeking his opinion again as she had done at his grandfather's house. "Not too bad," he said casually. "Your voice has — possibilities."

She turned from him angrily, knowing that she had never sung better in her life.

They crowded round Marcus, congratulating him on his playing, asking him if it was a hobby of his, and could he give them any hints on playing. Did he like country music and folk music and what did he think of their own compositions?

They were demonstrating that they had accepted him unreservedly. Carina, who should have been pleased, found herself resenting their acceptance. She felt, quite illogically, that in taking him so readily in to their circle, they were

40

conversely pushing her out.

"You seem to know quite a bit about music, Marcus," Luke said.

"I should do," Marcus answered dryly. "I'm a professional musician. I'm a B. Mus., a Bachelor of Music."

There was a stunned silence, then came the inevitable question, "What's your job?"

"A new one. I'm taking up my duties as head of the local school of music when the new term starts next month."

There was an awkward pause. Were the barriers going up again? Having let him in, would they now politely but firmly show him the door?

"Hear *me* sing, Marcus," said Olwen.

"No, me first," said Sandra.

They laughed, and Marcus with them. They had not shut him out again. Instead, they were offering him their respect yet accepting him at the same time as an equal.

Marcus turned to Seth. "I like your accompaniment to *Think of a life*. It's original, it's definitely got something."

"You think so?" Seth coloured with pleasure. "I thought it fitted the words. How did you like the words, Marcus?"

He glanced at the bright, expectant face of the girl who wrote them. "Not bad." He watched the eager brightness fade and just before she turned away, saw the lips drawn in with disappointment.

"Like to hear something I've written?" Dave asked.

"Go ahead," said Marcus.

Dave played his composition and received warm praise. Then Luke performed, followed by Seth accompanying Sandra. Marcus praised them, too.

Carina, sitting apart, heard it all, thinking miserably, "He's telling them all how good they are, yet nothing I do pleases him." She told herself how unfair he was to be so blindly prejudiced against her, no matter how well she performed.

Marcus looked at his watch and said it was time to go. He stood in front of Carina and said goodnight. She replied

41

without raising her eyes. The others saw Marcus to the door. Only Carina held back, sitting alone on a stool, plucking at the strings of her guitar.

"Come again, Marcus?" Seth asked.

"Kind of you to want me. I'd like to some time, provided Carina will forgive me."

Her head came up. "Forgive you for what?"

"Failing to be impressed by your possessions, your affluence, your worldly goods."

Their eyes held. "You'd be surprised," she said quietly, "how little I really have."

The deep seriousness in her voice was unmistakable, but he turned his back on it – literally – and the others laughed. "We told you, Marcus," they said, seeing him out, "pity the poor little rich girl."

"The day I pity a rich girl," Marcus's voice drifted back into the den, "will be the day the earth stops turning."

His car drove off and its noise faded into the distance. The others returned, and it was like a wedding reception after the bride and groom had gone. They flagged, they were restless, they fiddled with their instruments. But they did not produce any music – there was no one to listen, no expert to pronounce judgment on their performances.

Luke asked Carina how she had met Marcus de Verrier, and she told them.

"Why don't you like him?" Sandra demanded.

"Don't I like him?"

"You made it pretty obvious," Dave remarked.

Carina shrugged. "I haven't really got any feelings about him."

"He doesn't like you," Seth said. Carina was silent. "Never mind," Seth put his arm round her hunched shoulders, "we love you."

Dave put his arm round her, too, pulling her away from Seth. "What would we do without you?"

"Cupboard love," said Carina, with a weak smile,

42

shaking herself free of clinging arms. "It's my den you love, not me."

"If you really want to annoy the man," Olwen suggested, "enrol at the school of music next term."

Carina's fingers stilled, poised above the strings of her guitar. She looked up, her eyes bright.

"Now you've done it," said Seth, "you've put the idea into her head."

"She has," Carina said, her face floodlit with anticipation, "and I will."

There remained the obstacle of convincing her parents. But it was not as difficult as she had anticipated. They were hardened to her quixotic behaviour, to her unrelenting rejection through her adolescence and early adulthood of all the values they held most dear.

She had behind her two futile, wasted years, one spent on the doubtful fringes of art, the other dabbling, without even getting her fingers stained with duplicating ink, in office practice. Phyllis and Lloyd Ascott had asked each other helplessly and repeatedly, "What will she want to do next?"

If only, they complained to their acquaintances, she were as tractable as her sister Justine, the beautiful, the cherished, true child of her parents, who took after them in so many commendable ways. She was all they had dreamed a daughter should be.

When they had adopted Carina all those years ago, they had not imagined that the sad, big-eyed little girl they had taken to their hearts would develop such a complex, enigmatic personality. Her parents, although not in their social class, had been such pleasant people. This offspring of theirs must, the Ascotts were sure, be a throwback, a reversion by some playful trick of the genes, to the character of some distant and difficult ancestor.

It could not possibly be their fault, they argued. Hadn't they, her adoptive parents, given her everything a young

43

girl could possibly want, and more besides? A large personal allowance, a car, jewellery, a fine home? Thus they comforted each other and absolved themselves from all blame for the intractability of her nature.

So when Carina went to them and told them of her decision – that she was going to become a student again, this time at the school of music run by the local authority, they sighed, not with exasperation, as Carina had expected, but with relief. Not because it would cost them little financially – money was literally no object – but because as far as they were concerned, she could remain a student all her life, as long as she found some means of occupying her time. And time was something they could give her without limit, time in which to do whatever took her fancy.

Other girls in less fortunate financial circumstances would have had to stop fooling around and find a job. Carina, as far as they were concerned, need never do a stroke of work for the rest of her life, if that was how she wanted it. So they sighed with relief when she told them, because for the next nine months at least – three academic terms – they had the worry of what to do with her off their minds.

Soon Avery would be back – Lloyd Ascott had begun to wish he had never sent him away – and Avery would persuade her to marry him. Then they would give her an even bigger allowance, and she would be off their consciences for the rest of their lives, consciences as pure and uncontaminated as a surgeon's instruments, because of all they had given her since the day they carried her away from the children's home.

CHAPTER THREE

WHEN Ernest came to the door to welcome Carina in, her eyes were drawn as if by a powerful magnet up the stairs. Classical music, in stereo from the sound of it, drifted down.

Ernest led the way into the living-room, laughing at her worried frown. "He's in, lass, as you can hear. But he won't bite you, you know. He does get wild sometimes, always did, even as a young lad, but not that wild!" He sat in his favourite chair.

"You look smart, Mr. de Verrier."

Ernest thanked her kindly. "Never like to look dowdy. Tailoring was my trade, and old as I am I've never ceased to appreciate a good suit. Not that I've much money to spare for clothes nowadays, but my son, bless him, sees I don't go short. I only have a couple of suits, but they're good cloth and cut, I made sure of that before I bought them. Anyway," he sighed as though he were tired, "I always dress in my best when I go to hear young Carrie sing!"

"Sure you feel like it this evening, Mr. de Verrier? Not too tired?"

"Never too tired to listen to you, lass. Anyway, I'd never let you down. Even if I was on my deathbed, I'd get up off it to go and hear you!" He looked at her. "You always sing to me, don't you, lass?"

She nodded and smiled a little shyly. "Don't know what I'd do without you."

"Now if someone else said that, I'd say they didn't mean it. But you always mean what you say. I keep telling my grandson you're the most sincere and straightforward young woman I've ever known."

She picked at the strings of her guitar. "I bet he doesn't believe you."

Ernest's answer was indirect but revealing. "He's just plain obstinate, that one."

"When you talked about your son just now, did you mean Marcus's father?" Ernest nodded. "Where does he live?"

"In the west country, North Cornwall. With his wife, Edith. They've got a shop – musical instruments."

Her head came up. "So that's how Marcus knew how to play a guitar?"

Ernest laughed. "Not only a guitar. He's had a go at the whole flaming contents of that shop. Violins, flutes, drums, not to mention pianos, cymbals and trumpets."

She smiled. "A sort of one-man orchestra and soloist thrown in?" Ernest laughed again. "Mr. de Verrier? If I tell you something, will you keep it to yourself, at least for the moment?"

"Trust me, Carrie. I always keep your secrets."

"I've decided to enrol at the school of music next term."

"My grandson's school?" Ernest grew excited. "The one he's going to be head of? To do what, lass?"

"Learn the piano, perhaps, or the guitar. I can play them both, but I taught myself, so I thought I'd do even better if I had some expert tuition." There was a small, uncertain pause. "I don't know what else I could do. I've tried art and commerce and failed. I'm not much good at anything."

He could not let that pass. "But you can sing, Carrie, you can sing a treat."

She picked up her guitar, preparatory to leaving. "Perhaps, but I'd never make a living at it, would I?"

Carina helped Ernest on with his coat and the old man called upstairs that he was off. A shout in response meant that his grandson had heard.

It was a different old folks' club this time. Although it was in the next town, Ernest was known by its members. Wherever Carina sang, Ernest was there to hear. It was taken for granted that he was the young girl's grandfather, and this belief he never contradicted.

This particular club had benefited from the benign interest of the local authority, who had devoted a generous portion of the rates to building and equipping it. It had every comfort, even a tea bar. There was a platform at one end on which an entertainer could perform. There was even the luxury of a microphone plus a couple of speakers fixed to the walls near the back, a boon to members who were hard of hearing.

As soon as the audience was settled, Carina mounted the platform and sat on the chair which had been placed there for her. Someone turned down the lights and while she tuned her guitar there were a few last-minute coughs. The door at the back opened to admit one or two latecomers, but Carina was too absorbed to look up.

When there was silence, she began to sing. Her black hair fell forward over her cheeks. The skirt she wore was a deep blue, and swept the ground. The embroidered peasant blouse, together with the raven black of her hair, gave her appearance the touch of a gypsy. The pendant round her neck was a sapphire set in gold, and she wore long earrings to match.

She sang, and her songs were nostalgically of the past, hopefully of the future and sadly of the present. The wistful, haunting note in her voice made every song into a kind of lament, telling of the longings which lay deep in the secret places of her mind.

At the end of her performance there was the same sus-

47

pension of response, the same silence of full hearts and of people moved beyond words and even, momentarily, beyond applause.

Then it came, and with it the thunder of stamping feet. An encore was demanded and with her eyes on Ernest de Verrier, she sang his favourite, *Songs my mother taught me.*

It was over. The lights came up and Carina saw him, Marcus de Verrier, near the back, his face serious, his eyes on her. Instead of elation at the sight of him, she began to fret. Why had he come? To act as an irritant? To laugh at the "poor little rich girl" for handing out gifts to the needy in the form of nostalgia, sentiment and the stirring up of long-forgotten memories? Indignation brought the colour to her cheeks, and life into her legs.

She stepped down from the platform and went to Ernest's side. He drew her down and kissed her cheek. "It was grand, lass," he whispered. People spoke to her, thanked her and told her to be sure to come again.

"You've got something rare, dear," said a plump, smiling old lady. "It's almost like you reach out and touch us. It's not just your youth and your looks, it's something else. Keep it, dear, whatever you do, don't lose it."

Marcus, who had come to stand beside Carina, heard the woman's words. Carina would not ask him this time how she had sung. She would not let him know that his opinion of her mattered. It was these people she had come to entertain, and if they were pleased and touched and even, now and then, moved to tears, that was all she asked.

"Coming home, Mr. de Verrier?" she invited, ignoring the grandson.

But far from being ignored, the grandson staked his claim. "I shall take my grandfather home, Carina."

Apart from a slight stiffening of her spinal column, Carina showed no awareness of his presence. She helped Ernest from his seat and kept a possessive hand on his arm.

"Coming with me, Grandfather?" Marcus asked.

48

"*I* usually take Mr. de Verrier back," Carina said coldly.

Ernest looked from one to the other, sensing the conflict and feeling the tug inside him. What should he do? Submit to the pull of the family and go with his grandson? Or give in to the young girl beside him, the tightness of her lips betraying her almost obsessive fear of being rejected?

He saw the girl's eyes meet his grandson's with a challenge which was returned in full. He saw the relaxed possessiveness of the young man, a possessiveness born of the knowledge that the person they were fighting over was his own flesh and blood. He looked again at the girl, her eyes beginning to yield, her body starting to sag, the girl with no family of her own, but grafted like a transplant, on to another, and who had felt years ago the beginnings of rejection by the "host".

Carina turned away, leaving the victor to claim the prize.

"I'll go with Carina," Ernest said, his eyes uplifted in a silent plea to his grandson to try to understand. "I usually do."

Ernest followed her to the door. He wished he could tell his grandson about this girl he had befriended, her secrets, her uncertainties, the tragedy of her childhood which had had so profound an effect on her personality. But he had sworn to keep her secrets and keep them he would, until his dying day.

Ernest went upstairs when they arrived home, and Carina followed the usual pattern by making a pot of tea. She hoped desperately that on his return Marcus would go up to his room. But he came into the house and made straight for the kitchen. He looked at the tray, looked at her and raised his eyebrows at the significant omission of a cup and saucer for himself and added them to the others.

He opened a tin of biscuits, put one in his mouth and with a miming action offered her the tin, unable to speak because of the biscuit between his teeth.

This made her laugh and she took one, thanking him. His hands were free now, so he leaned back against a cupboard and crunched his biscuit. He said appreciatively, "M'm, coated with chocolate. I suppose the biscuits you eat at home are coated with gold?"

"Yes," she answered with a grin, "and we eat off gold plate and drink out of Sèvres porcelain."

"And you're waited on by a retinue, not to say a regiment, of servants who pander to your every whim?"

"Well," she poured the boiling water into the teapot, "if you can call three a regiment, yes."

"You mean you really do have three servants?"

They were back again on the old footing, enemies on a familiar battleground, class warfare without end.

"Two of them are part-time," she said, on the defensive at once, "and come in daily. Only the housekeeper lives in."

"Don't fall over backwards being apologetic. It's not my business. It doesn't matter to me one jot if you're waited on like royalty." There was a barbed silence. He finished his biscuit, dusted his hands and said, "If it's not a rude question, what is your father's occupation?"

Before answering him, she carried the tray into the living-room where Ernest was waiting patiently in his armchair. He put down the newspaper and sat himself upright, accepting his tea gratefully.

As Carina gave Marcus his, she asked, "Ever heard of Ascott clothes?"

"Vaguely. For women? I think I've seen them advertised in Sunday magazine supplements. High-class stuff, aren't they, which only the best people can afford?" She nodded. "Ah, I see." He sat down, leaned back and stretched out his legs. "Now it all fits." He looked her over and drank some tea. "You're hardly a walking advertisement for your father's styles, are you? What does he do with you when important guests come to dinner to talk business? Push you under the table?"

She laughed. "He doesn't need to. I always absent myself. My mother and my sister are so decorative no one notices I'm missing."

"You don't consider yourself 'decorative'?"

"No." She picked up her guitar and played it softly. "My appearance has never worried me greatly."

"And you with a father in the fashion game? You must be the bane of their lives."

"I am," she murmured, her mind on the jumble of music she was producing. "They despaired of me long ago. Justine, my beautiful sister, reigns supreme in my family." A shadow veiled her face, no more than a wisp of cloud passing across the sun on a summer's day.

"Sing to us, lass," came the familiar persuasive plea.

"No," said the grandson, "listen to this instead."

He replaced his empty cup on the tray, pulled from his pocket a portable cassette recorder and set it going. It was a recording of Carina's performance that evening at the old people's club.

The pensive, almost melancholy note, the haunting magic of the voice had been captured and held, like a wild creature against its will, weaving the same spell, closing the eyes and reaching down into the depths of those who were listening. The entire performance was there, and Ernest, his face alight with pleasure, a tremor in his voice, thanked his grandson for what he had done. "Keep it, Marcus, don't rub it off. Keep it so I can hear it again and again. I told you she was good, didn't I? Tell her she's good, Marcus. She doesn't believe me. She thinks I only say it to please her."

His grandson snapped the cassette recorder shut and slipped it into his pocket. He sat back, folding his arms, and contemplated the girl on the footstool. She was looking up at him, her fingers resting against the strings of her guitar, her whole body waiting, waiting for his verdict. Her eyes were bright, her lips parted in anticipation of his praise.

He seemed to be turning over in his mind what he was

51

going to say. When he did speak, what he said was carefully noncommittal. "It was a good performance."

For Carina it was not enough. "But my singing, what about that?"

He still did not give a direct answer. "What was it that old lady said to you? 'You've got something rare. It's almost as if you can reach out and touch us!' " He finished, still using the old lady's words, and with that she had to be satisfied. "Keep it, Carina, that 'something rare'. Don't lose it, whatever you do."

The school of music was a modern, purpose-built structure, standing within the precincts of the town's technical college. On the day Carina enrolled as a student, it was full of young people milling around aimlessly, filling in forms at tables and wandering in and out of rooms.

Carina consulted a woman at the enquiries desk and was asked which instruments she intended to study. She didn't know, she said, she would like advice.

"Go to the first floor and see one of the teachers," she was told.

The first floor was packed with students, too. Curiosity made her pull up sharply in front of a door bearing metal holders, into which had been slotted a typewritten card. "Marcus de Verrier," it said, followed by a formidable list of letters, presumably the qualifications the man had collected on his journey through the music jungle, and displayed as proudly as a hunter of wild animals fixes his captured heads to the wall.

Carina hesitated, wondering whether to knock, and trying to imagine whether Marcus, Ernest's grandson, was anything like Marcus de Verrier, head of the school of music, when the door opened. Marcus emerged. Ernest's grandson he might be, but it was definitely the head of the music school who came out.

He was so preoccupied, his eyes, like his mind being focussed on work and not on personalities, he did not notice

52

the girl in the corridor until she called his name.

"Mr. de Verrier?"

He stopped in his tracks and turned to face the source of the voice. It seemed to take him a few seconds to pull his mind down from the heights and concentrate on the girl – some irritating female, his expression said – who, rabbit-like, had burrowed into his thoughts. When he saw who it was, there was no pleasure in his recognition. He looked instead as if he would like to reach for a gun and put an end to that particular rabbit's existence.

He took aim. "What the devil," he snapped, "are you doing here?"

"I've come to enrol, Mr. de Verrier."

He got her in his sights. He walked slowly back to confront her. "To *what*?"

"Enrol. As a music student."

There it was again, the uncertainty, the fear of repulse, the feeling that dogged her night and day. The slightest setback, the mildest reprimand could spark it off, and in no time at all it was enveloping her as if she were alight. Ernest would have read the signs, sensed the increase in pulse rate, seen the pressing together of the lips.

But the grandson, with no such knowledge of her character, with his prejudice and hostility towards all he thought she stood for, narrowed his eyes. He fired a round. "Run out of ideas as to what to do with yourself next? First commerce, then art, now music?"

"But, Mr. de Verrier, it's not like that . . ."

He had hit the target, but the rabbit still survived. In fact, it stood there petrified.

"Come into my office." She obeyed and he closed the door. "Tell me, what exactly is your aim in coming here? I suppose you know I have the right to veto the admission of any student I consider undesirable?"

"But, Mr. de Verrier," why couldn't she keep her voice steady? "how can you say I'm undesirable? I've done nothing –"

"That, Miss Ascott, is the point. You have done nothing. Your whole life, as far as I can see, has been spent fooling around acting the perpetual student, drifting aimlessly from one department to another, with no genuine interest in the subjects you have studied, and with no particular career in mind."

There was a short, tense silence. She asked, her throat tight, "Are you telling me you're refusing to allow me to enrol?" He did not reply and she went on, "Music is the only thing left. There's nothing else. Music is my life, it's all I really care about." He still did not speak, so she turned hopelessly to the door.

His voice followed her. Was it gloating? "Money can't buy everything, you know."

She swung round, her eyes large with fury. "*Money!* Money is all you can think about. It obsesses you, because of what happened in your past." His eyebrows rose as if asking, how did she know? "Your grandfather told me. I know you hate me because of my background. All right, hate me as much as you like, but at least give me the chance to prove myself. If I fail, you can throw me out. If I succeed, you'll take the credit. Either way you win. You simply can't lose."

He seemed to capitulate, but even so he did it reluctantly. "Which instruments did you have in mind to specialise in?"

She shrugged, but that proved to be a mistake, because as he watched the action, his eyes hardened. She supposed the careless movement had annoyed him because with it she had, in his eyes, dismissed the entire world of music as of no consequence.

She answered, "The piano, perhaps, and the guitar."

"You can forget the guitar. Take singing."

"*Forget* the guitar? When I love it so much?"

"We teach the classical guitar here, and that requires a very different technique and touch from the one you use in

54

playing your kind of music. So I repeat, you can forget the guitar. You would not make a classical guitarist even if you studied it to the end of your days."

She had to concede that he was probably right. "But there's still the piano. I can play that."

"You have a piano at home on which to practise?"

"Yes. A grand piano."

He named a famous make. Had she got that? he asked, with a tight, sarcastic smile. When she nodded, his eyes glinted as if he had scored a point against her.

Carina flushed, and said, on the defensive again, "My father knew of my interest in the piano, so he bought it for me."

"And it goes without saying that for you he bought the most expensive, the very best?"

"Why not? He could afford it."

"Why not, indeed? Why not spoil his daughter, his beautiful daughter, by giving her everything she wants?"

"You've got the wrong daughter. I'm not the beautiful one. That's Justine, my sister."

Ernest de Verrier would have recognised the sincerity of her statement, but his grandson did not. "False modesty, Miss Ascott, cuts no ice with me." He glanced at his watch. "So you want to wish yourself on me as a student? Since you must take two subjects, make it piano and singing."

"But I can't study *singing*. I haven't got a good enough voice."

"Don't you think that I'm the best judge of that?"

"But you've only heard me sing folk songs and a ballad or two."

"Even if I had only heard you sing up and down the scales a few times, I would still have been able to judge whether or not you had a voice worth developing. If you work and practise and study conscientiously, there's no doubt in my mind that you would succeed as a singer.

There's a latent quality in your voice that, given the right teaching and treatment, could take you to great heights."

Her eyes came open. "With what end in view?".

"Opera."

"*Opera?* You're surely exaggerating!"

He looked at his watch again, with some impatience. "Go and enrol. Time will tell whether I'm 'exaggerating' or not."

When Phyllis and Lloyd Ascott heard of their daughter's decision to study singing, and of the direction in which her studies might one day lead, they showed themselves to be mildly pleased.

As she left them to go upstairs to her room, Carina had the feeling that deep down they were sceptical. They had, of course, heard it all before. First there had been office practice – it would lead to a good secretarial post, she had told them. Then had come art – there was no knowing where that might take her. Now it was opera. She supposed they simply could not visualize her, the *enfant terrible* they had adopted so many years ago, fitting into the somewhat conventional role of a prima donna.

"Let her go on with it," Phyllis said to her husband, thinking Carina was out of earshot, "and get it out of her system. It won't take long – a few months, perhaps. By then Avery will have returned and they can be married. Then she'll settle down to being a good wife and mother and forget all this nonsense of commerce and art and music."

"I wonder," Lloyd remarked, "if I could bring Avery back earlier than I had planned?"

"Darling," his wife replied, "if you could, for heaven's sake, do. It would solve so many problems. We could have an engagement party at Christmas and they could marry next Easter. A spring wedding would be wonderful."

So that's what they're planning, Carina thought indignantly, as she went upstairs. Let them plan, if it makes them happy. But they're wasting their time. She ran up to her room to practise the songs she would sing the next time she visited the old people's club.

On her first day as a music student, Carina found herself caught irresistibly by the rhythm of the place. She felt stimulated as if there were at last something in her life worth living for. She mingled with the other students, rejoicing in the fact that she shared with them a common love – that of music. She belonged among them and, as long as Marcus did not harden his heart against her and throw her out, among them she would remain. What was more, this time she intended to stay the course.

A notice in the entrance hall instructed all first-year students to go on arrival to the hall, where the head of the school of music would address them. With the others Carina drifted through the double entrance doors and chose a seat a few rows from the front.

They stared about them, trying to familiarise themselves with the strange surroundings, looking towards the stage, which was hidden from view by green velvet curtains, and watching apprehensively as if a pantomime ogre were about to emerge. They gazed up at the spotlights fixed to the walls, and contemplated the sky beyond the high-reaching windows.

There was a disturbance behind the velvet curtains, but it was no frightening ogre who appeared. It was Marcus de Verrier who pushed his way through the opening. He was brisk, self-assured and completely devoid of self-consciousness, like a man accustomed to facing an audience. He glanced round, his eyes scanning the eager, upturned faces, passed over Carina as though he had never seen her before and began talking.

He gave a brief outline of the work of the school, spoke of the many opportunities which existed for all students, provided they worked hard at their chosen subjects. He touched on the aims of the courses they were taking, and how they must not stagnate and return year after year, but must pass their examinations and move on to the more specialised training they would receive at the London schools of music.

When his talk was over, he came down the steps into the auditorium, walked along the centre gangway and paused at the end of Carina's row. "Miss Ascott?" he said.

The other students looked at her curiously, wondering how it was the head of the school knew her name and why she had been singled out for special attention. Did he have to be so tactless? she thought.

"See me in my office in five minutes," he said, and went on his way.

When Carina tapped on his door and entered the room, he rose, handing her a piece of paper. "Your timetable. There are more than the usual numbers of free periods. I see from your enrolment form that you have passed most of the compulsory examinations which many students coming here for the first time have not."

She frowned at his tone. "Yes, I have."

He smiled ironically. "Forgive the surprise, but I assumed, from all I've heard about your chequered and unproductive career to date, that your academic achievements had been nil."

She flushed. "Even I, Mr. de Verrier, dull as I am, can benefit from an expensive education. Money, as you say, can't buy everything. For instance, it can't buy brilliance, but it can buy the means of shovelling knowledge into even the thickest of heads, even to the point of ensuring that that head retains the knowledge at least long enough to pass an exam."

He murmured to the papers on his desk, "As my grandfather says, 'she bites when provoked.' "

She frowned again. "I'm sorry. I didn't mean to be rude."

"I'm sure you didn't. An expensive education is a veritable breeding ground for good manners, if nothing else."

She was silent, waiting for his next move.

"I suppose," he said, "you're wondering why I asked you, out of all the new students, to come and see me?"

"Knowing your opinion of me, probably for a pep talk."

"Not so much that, as a directive. You've enrolled in my music school. You're not here for fun or to pass the time as you did in the other subjects you dabbled in. You're going to work – damned hard. I have no time for failures, and you are going to succeed. Right?"

"I can only do my best, Mr. de Verrier."

"Your 'best' is not good enough, Carina. Is there a place where you can practise at home?"

"I told you, we have a piano."

"I know you have a piano." He was obviously trying to be patient. "What I meant was, is the atmosphere right? Will your parents be sympathetic? Will they be able to stand the monotony of the sounds made by a singer practising? Will they grumble and put you off, or be long-suffering and thus encourage you?"

"The piano is in the lounge. Besides being my 'toy', it's a showpiece."

He frowned. "You've given me the answer I expected, which means you will have to sacrifice some of your evenings and return here to practise."

"But," she said, dismayed, "I'm not going to take the subject all that seriously." She could not have made a more damaging statement if she had tried.

He came round to stand in front of her, his anger under control – but only just. "Look here, Carina, isn't it time you grew up? Isn't it time you stopped drifting aimlessly, like an abandoned ship in a storm? If you study singing – under my direction – you will take it more seriously than you have ever taken anything in your life. Otherwise," he rooted for her enrolment card amongst the papers on his desk and found it, "I might as well do this. Now." He made a tearing motion with his fingers.

Her hand shot out to stop him. She felt as if he were about to rip her out of his life like a torn-out month from a

59

calendar. That enrolment card was the embodiment of her future. If he tore it up, she might as well stop living here and now.

He smiled. He had got the reaction he wanted.

CHAPTER FOUR

AT dinner that evening, Phyllis and Lloyd showed a measured amount of interest in their elder daughter's first day as a music student. It was measured in the sense that it had been calculated to the exact quantity required – no more, no less – to let her know how deep was their regard for her, despite the fact that she was not of their flesh as Justine was, and that she shared an equal place with their "real" daughter in their affections. They had, after all, gone out of their way to show their love – hadn't they plied her with gift after gift?

Irritated beyond words by her parents' studied interest in her first day at the school of music – although later she told herself she could not really blame them, they had had to listen to accounts of so many "first days" as a student – she roared her sports car round to Ernest de Verrier's.

At an upstairs window Marcus flicked a net curtain aside at the screech of brakes. With her guitar under her arm she walked in and received from Ernest the welcome she had been waiting for. She basked in it like a rheumatic patient revelling in the warmth of a sun lamp.

He listened, his shadowed eyes glowing, as she told him how good it was to be surrounded by music all day, seeing it on paper in front of your eyes, hearing it in your head and in your ears from other people's lessons. She did not, however, mention Marcus's pep talk. Somehow, the fact

61

that he had felt it necessary to give it to her and to no one else still rankled.

Marcus appeared at the door. "You here *again*?" The question was injected with resentment, but instead of poisoning relations between them as it was probably intended to do, Carina showed herself to be tolerably resistant to it.

She turned a wide-eyed unbelieving face towards him and asked, "You can't surely be *jealous*?"

Ernest laughed, slapping his thigh. "He could be, lass, he could be that."

"But, Marcus –" she stopped, frowned, and asked, "Do you mind if I call you that?"

"At home, no," he answered, "as long as you don't carry your informality over into the school of music." He sat down. "You were about to say?"

"I was going to say how could anyone who 'belongs' be jealous of someone who doesn't 'belong'?"

"Don't be silly, Carrie," Ernest said, surprisingly abrupt. "You belong here as much as he does."

She shook her head, her fingers plucking at the guitar strings, her eyes not seeing them. "I don't," she whispered, "belong to anyone."

"In the romantic sense, I suppose you mean," said Marcus.

Ernest and Carina exchanged glances, but no one answered Marcus.

"I suppose," Marcus said into the silence, "you're off on one of your folk-singing jaunts this evening?"

"Not tonight," his grandfather replied.

"Then why the guitar?" Marcus motioned to the instrument with his hand – which was near enough to touch it – and Carina held it to her as if she were nursing a beloved pet. He saw the reflex action and laughed.

Every time he came near, she felt the pull of him, like the wizard of child mythology extending his fingers and saying *Abracadabra*, and her guitar would disappear in a cloud of smoke. The feeling was assuming the proportions of a nightmare.

"I think," Carina said, forcing her tone to be light, "you've got designs on my guitar. Every time you see it, I get the feeling you want to take it from me."

He leaned back, his hand tantalisingly near hers. "I have got designs on it," he said softly. "One day I *shall* take it away from you – for good."

Carina had not been looking forward to her first singing lesson with Marcus. It was timetabled for the last day of her first week.

When she went into the practice room he was not there. The room was small and intimate, almost cell-like in its bareness. There was a grand piano, a stool and a chair. Some music stood on the stand over the piano keys and she turned the pages, trying to rationalise the tension away from her muscles.

He swept into the room as though his body was trying to keep pace with his thoughts. He motioned her away from the piano, indicating that he wanted her to stand next to it, but facing him. There was a tension in him, too, but of a different sort, a tension of anticipation, of alertness and the consciousness of a job to be done.

He ran his fingers over the keys, listening to the result as if his ear found agreeable even the sound produced by the rising and falling of the scales.

"Now," he said, relaxing as if he were temporarily satisfied, like a man who had slaked his thirst with a long reviving drink, "back to the drawing board." His fingers still rested on the piano keys as if reluctant to lose touch with them, as her fingers felt constantly for the strings of her guitar. "You can forget all the knowledge you have acquired in the past about singing. I imagine you are self-taught, that one day you discovered that, by opening your mouth and using your throat in a certain way, you could produce a pleasant sound?"

She laughed and nodded, relaxing momentarily but tensing up again. He looked her over as if he knew exactly was going on in her mind – and body. He stood and faced her, took her clasped hands in his, lifted them, opened them and felt the moisture on her palms.

He looked at her inquiringly. "What's the matter? I don't bite, you know."

"I can't help being nervous."

Her hands were still resting in his. "I thought that the expensive, exclusive education through which you were processed, packaged and delivered was intended to impart, amongst other things, a poise guaranteed to carry you through every conceivable situation, even to facing an earthquake with calm and equanimity."

She removed her hands. "It didn't work with me. I told you, not only was I not 'finished', I wasn't even 'begun'."

"You were the one who got away? Your father should have asked for his money back." He saw the strain in her eyes. "Pity. You could have done with that poise." He sat down again. "A good singer needs nervous tension, but a tension which is controlled so that it does not itself take control." He played a few bars on the piano as if the temptation was too great to be resisted. "But take comfort," he told the piano keys, "a cool head, a cold heart and a frigid, passionless personality never did combine to make a great singer." He looked up, an eyebrow raised. "Are you frigid, Carina?"

He was getting too personal. "I – I don't know." The uncertain frown came and went under his provocative regard.

"So your passions have never been put to the test? Despite that ring you wear?"

"I told you, it's not an engagement ring."

"It's as near as makes no difference. Be honest."

"I don't see that this is relevant. I don't see that it's any business of yours."

"I'm sorry," he said, gently now, "but it is. You see, a

64

teacher – a good teacher – must get to know his pupil as a man – or a woman. He has to interest himself in the student's way of life, his character, his background. The teaching of singing is a most personal act. It is not a business arrangement. The atmosphere between the two of us must be friendly and trusting." He stood again and looked into the disturbing brown eyes, saw the doubt and withdrawal which his words had produced, like a baby flinching from the overtures of a well meaning but over-hearty adult. "Both of us have a lot to overcome – prejudice, bias in one form or another, resentment, even. If you and I are going to succeed – I in teaching, you in learning – we must leave outside this room the antagonisms we feel towards each other. Even if we hate each other outside, in here and in all our professional and artistic contacts there must all the time be a reciprocity and an unfailing trust between us. Have I your trust?"

She looked into his eyes and saw the integrity there, the artist inside him reaching out and trying to make contact. She saw Ernest de Verrier looking out of his eyes, too, and the strong family likeness she had noticed before proved a magnet she could not resist. Yes, she answered, she trusted him.

"Good. Now, back to basics. You're a new student, and as such where your vocal apparatus is concerned, you're like a blind man going into a strange room. Everything in it is unfamiliar, the furniture, the fixtures, the feel of the carpet and the upholstery. You wouldn't go blundering into such a place, you'd feel your way, you would walk carefully and with caution. You understand?" She nodded. "But before you can even sing a note, you must learn to breathe. A singer breathes with his lungs, with his ribs, not with his throat."

He cupped his hands and fitted them round her diaphragm, pressing against her ribs. She tightened at his touch and her instinct was to pull away.

There was a flash of anger in his eyes, like the flare of a

match, but he had it under control within seconds. "I'm not making a pass at you, Carina. I'm merely doing my job."

She coloured deeply. "I'm sorry, Mr. de Verrier, but the movement was purely instinctive." She laughed uncomfortably, finding the intimate touch of his hands around her body almost unbearable. She finished weakly, "Conditioned reflex."

He considered her thoughtfully. "To me, or to any man?" She did not answer, so he told her, "Take a breath, expand your lungs and with your ribs push my hands as far away as you can."

She complied, feebly at first, then gaining strength at each attempt. "Good," he said, removing his hands at last. "Practise that at home regularly each day."

Towards the end of the lesson she flagged. She had sung only a few notes – to her ears a feeble and unsatisfactory sound – but she felt as exhausted as if she had given an evening's performance to a demanding audience.

He sensed her tiredness and brought the lesson to a sudden halt. "It's early, but you've had enough. You can go."

He had become abrupt, as cut off from her as an aircraft rising up and dwindling to a speck in the sky. The lesson was over, so relations between them were back to normal. He began to play – the piece was by Beethoven, but she did not recognise it – and his mind was totally on the music. She lingered beside him and he looked up at her impatiently.

"May I listen?" she asked.

He shrugged as if it were immaterial to him whether she stayed or not. She sat, hands clasped, eyes on his talented, restless fingers, hearing the mastery of his touch, the perfection of his playing, feeling his concentration and becoming part of it.

Knowing he was oblivious to her, she looked at his handsome profile and saw his absolute involvement with the music he was producing. She knew that if there were ever a woman with whom he might one day consent to share his life, that woman would also have to share his love of music.

There would be no half measures. He would demand from her his own complete and unequivocal dedication. She wondered with a tinge of pain if such a woman existed who would ever hope to come up to his high standards. She had no doubt about one thing — the woman he eventually chose would be as far removed from the Carina Ascotts of this world as the earth is from the sun.

After the walk and the group music session that weekend, Carina took Seth upstairs to her bedroom. They had a new song in mind and wanted to work on it. They went into the house through the kitchen, and Carina hoped they would get upstairs unobserved. There was no love lost between her parents and her friends.

Seth was always reluctant to enter the Ascott residence. Its opulence repelled him and even the kitchen gave him a feeling of inferiority. It was a characterless room, clinically clean, without the faintest trace about it of the homeliness or disorder usually found in the kitchens of ordinary families. Whenever he left the house, even after a short stay, he felt as if a great weight had rolled off his back. But he liked Carina, and he only went into the place to please her.

Seth's hand was in hers as they left the kitchen and she was pulling him behind her. In their other hands they were holding their guitars. First they met Lloyd, crossing the hall from the dining-room to the drawing-room. He nodded at Seth and closed the door on them. Then they met Phyllis at the foot of the stairs. Her eyes rested on their linked hands and she gave Seth the strained lady-of-the-manor smile she reserved for all Carina's friends.

Carina and Seth sat side by side on the bed. There were armchairs, but in those they could not get close enough to work together properly.

"How's this for a beginning?" Carina asked. *"The con-*

science of the world is on my mind, There's no peace in myself that I can find."

"Good," said Seth, his fingers already feeling for a suitable tune to put to the words. He committed some notes to paper and worked over the sequence for some time. "Go on," he said at last.

She repeated the first two lines and added, *"Murdered innocents, crying wives, rattling machine guns, plunging knives . . ."*

Seth held up his hand and played over a series of phrases, writing them down. "Carry on."

"I want to sit down here and cry each time one of these brave people die. Isn't there anyone going to say it's got to come to an end some day."

Inspired, eyes shining, Seth finished the accompaniment, then played the whole piece through. Softly, adding the sound of her guitar to his, Carina began to sing, picking up the tune as she went. Then she repeated it all.

As she sang this time, she tried to remember what Marcus had taught her about breathing and about the importance of the correct enunciation of the vowels, but found she could not incorporate what she had learned with the singing of this kind of song. The two just did not go together, so she abandoned her attempt to put theory into practice and sang in the old way. She felt a twinge of conscience, but no more. She would sing for Marcus in the way he wanted, but at home she would sing how she liked.

The song, its birth pangs over, hung upon the air, as disturbing as the cries of a new-born baby. They put aside their guitars and looked at each other, the triumph of achievement lighting up their faces. Seth's hand covered hers, then he pulled her to him and experimentally found her lips with his. It was the first time they had kissed and to Carina it was not unpleasant.

He took her lack of resistance as encouragement and pushed her back until she was lying with her head on the pillows. They kissed again. His hand moved and touched her, but she tightened up and thrust it away with the frenzied fear of someone hitting out at a bee before it settled and stung.

He sat up at once, red, uncomfortable, mumbling, "I'm sorry."

She was sorry, too, for having humiliated him and that it had ever happened. His personality clicked back into place, like a ballpoint pen retracting. He picked up his guitar and plucked at the strings. Carina retrieved hers and did the same. They returned to their work as if nothing had happened.

"Are you frigid?" Marcus had asked. "I don't know," she had replied. She still did not know the answer.

Besides receiving individual tuition in piano playing from a nondescript-looking woman called Miss Ringstead, in class Carina studied harmony, counterpoint and the history of music. Because she had passed a number of the statutory examinations while still at school, she had a large amount of free time.

One morning, having nothing better to do, she wandered about the building, listening to the jumble of sounds creeping out into the corridor from behind closed doors. Marcus caught her at it.

"Why aren't you working, Miss Ascott?" he asked sharply.

"I have a free period, Mr. de Verrier."

"You seem to have an inordinately large number of free periods, judging by the frequency with which I've seen you hanging about doing nothing."

Was he spying on her, trying to catch her out and find an excuse for removing her from the music school?

"I'm sorry." She looked away, uncertain as she always was under his keen gaze. "It's just that there are a lot of empty spaces in my timetable."

"Let me see it."

Unnerved by his abruptness, she fumbled in her briefcase

69

and produced the piece of paper. He looked at it, looked at his watch and said accusingly, "You should be at your German class."

"It seems a bit silly, Mr. de Verrier, when I already speak it fluently. French, too."

"Oh? How did that come about?"

She fastened and unfastened the catch on her briefcase. "As a result of my travels abroad over the years with my parents. And I was at a finishing school on the Continent, remember."

She had reminded him of her background – but surely he never forgot it? – and in doing so had raked back to life the embers of his cynicism.

"Ah, yes, the establishment that gives the extra polish so necessary to daughters of the rich." He handed her the timetable. "What about Italian? For opera you need to have a working knowledge of Italian."

She shook her head.

"Thank God there's something you don't know." He took the timetable back from her, got out a pen, scored through German and French and went into his room, telling her to follow. He consulted the prospectus to find out when classes in Italian were held and filled in some spaces on her timetable. She thanked him and prepared to leave.

"Before you go," she turned back to face him, "Miss Ringstead tells me you're making slow progress with the piano. With the showpiece of a piano such as you have at home, you should surely be approaching the genius class by now?"

"A good piano doesn't necessarily produce a good player, Mr. de Verrier."

"Well said, Miss Ascott," his tone had softened a little, "just as a good voice does not necessarily make a good singer. Now, you want something to do? Find an empty room and spend the rest of your free time practising the piano."

She sighed and nodded. Her reluctance appeared to irritate him and he snapped, "Tired of music already, Miss Ascott? That's a little early, isn't it, even for you? The year you seem to have allocated to each of your dabblings in miscellaneous subjects isn't up yet by a long way."

In her mind a door slammed, shutting in her self-restraint. Another flew open and anger stampeded out like children let out of school. Her colour rose, her eyes blazed. "Your prejudices, as usual, are showing, Mr. de Verrier. I resent your bias against me, your inference that I'm a drifter. You base your accusation on what you heard my friends say that day you came with us on our walk through the forest. On hearsay only, you've judged me and found me wanting. Right from the start you've never given me a chance to prove myself or – or anything else!" Under his scrutiny her rhetoric had run out, leaving her speechless. She sensed that she had not moved him one iota from his preconceived opinions about her.

"Tell me, Miss Ascott," he flipped through a music score on his desk, "was it not true what they said about you that day, about your trying first one subject, then another?"

"Of course it was true, but –" 'But you only know half the story,' she was going to say, but he interrupted.

"Then what are you grumbling about? You've proved my point for me."

"I never thought," she said quietly, "that a grandson of Ernest de Verrier could be so bigoted and so – so lacking in compassion."

She could say no more. She could not engage in a bitter and acrimonious quarrel with the head of the music school.

The door behind her stood open, inviting her to leave. She accepted its invitation and closed it quietly, shutting in the silence.

Carina sought solace on the footstool in Ernest de Verrier's living-room. Her guitar was, as usual, on her lap.

"How are you making out with Marcus?" Ernest asked. "He never mentions you."

71

"People don't usually talk about things that displease them. They put them to the back of their minds." She heard footsteps overhead and lowered her voice. "Marcus doesn't like me, Mr. de Verrier." It was said without emotion, as though it were a fact of life which had to be faced.

Ernest stared straight ahead at the picture of himself and his late wife taken amongst the flowers in the back garden. "I don't see how anyone can *dis*like you, Carrie."

"Ask Marcus. He knows."

After a prolonged silence, Ernest said, "He seems to have found himself a lady-friend."

The world reeled round Carina's head as though she had received a blow. She closed her eyes until it stopped, telling herself it was the stuffiness of the room ."Who is she?"

"Some woman at the college. Piano teacher, name of Faith. Can't remember her surname."

"It wouldn't be – Ringstead?"

"That's it. He brought her here the other evening. Said they'd come to work. Mousey-looking creature, no life in her."

What was it Marcus had said? 'Miss Ringstead tells me you're making slow progress on the piano.' Yes, Miss Ringstead would, because Miss Ringstead didn't like her, either.

"I've got a new song, Mr. de Verrier. Like to hear it?"

Ernest shifted and came to life. "Carry on, lass."

First she played a few bars of the music as an introduction, then she began to sing, softly at first, her voice growing louder and richer as the feeling inside her increased.

> *"The conscience of the world is on my mind,*
> *There's no peace in myself that I can find,*
> *Murdered innocents, crying wives,*
> *Rattling machine guns, plunging knives;*
> *I want to sit down here and cry*
> *Each time one of those brave people die.*
> *Isn't there anyone going to say*
> *It's got to come to an end some day?"*

"Who wrote that?" She swung round to face the speaker, resenting the intrusion and showing it.

"Seth wrote the music. I wrote the words." She watched Marcus advance into the room with as much pleasure as a criminal watching a policeman come to the house to take her away.

"*You* wrote them?"

"Yes. What of it?" *Had* she committed some crime?

"Whoever heard," he sat down, "of a daughter of the rich having a political conscience?"

Ernest winced as though his grandson had struck him. "Don't speak to her like that, Marcus. The words were good."

"Who said they weren't?"

"There was nothing political about them," Carina protested. "It's just a case of common humanity."

"And compassion, of which I, of course, have none." So her accusation that afternoon had gone home. "Once again, to my astonishment, I find myself in agreement with the sentiments expressed. Astonished also that they could come from someone like you."

"Can't you credit me with *any* sincerity," she cried, "with any finer feelings?"

He refused to be caught by the palpable honesty in those troublesome eyes. He turned to baiting as a form of self-defence. "The words were a freak of chance."

"And the other poem I wrote?" she challenged. "Was that a 'freak', too?"

His smile was nicely calculated to irritate. "Yes." He considered her. "You know what you are? A do-gooder." He put up his hand to stop her protests. "Don't get me wrong. Not in the sense that the women of your class, your mother's social circle, are do-gooders – let me finish – I don't condemn them. A very commendable way to spend their spare time. I mean a do-gooder in the sense that you hand out, not charity or food to the needy, but visions of a better future to gullible people. You're playing at being a

73

revolutionary. With your background, how could it be otherwise?"

"You're being unkind, Marcus," his grandfather warned, "you don't know how unkind."

Marcus gave her a sceptical look. "Never let it be said that I could ever bring myself to be unkind to Miss Carina Ascott, heiress to the Ascott millions." He gave a low, almost reverent bow. "Please accept my sincere apologies, Miss Ascott."

He returned to his room.

Carina floundered at her next singing lesson. Marcus asked her if she had been practising the breathing exercises. Once again he tested the power of her diaphragm muscles by asking her to push his hands apart as he held them clamped round her ribs. It was the touch of his hands that threw her off balance from the start. She tensed, and he must have felt it because he told her to relax, but she could only shake her head.

"Never tighten your throat when breathing," he advised. "You must allow your voice to vibrate on the soundboard here," he touched her forehead and her face just below her eyes. She flinched, but he let it pass. His fingers rested on her lips. "Mould your words with these. Keep them mobile." She drew in her lips so that he had to remove his fingers.

He frowned. "Good God, girl, what's the matter? Every time I touch you you flinch away. Am I so repulsive?"

She shook her head helplessly. How could she explain to him how his touch made her feel?

He brought the conversation back to safer ground. He moved away saying, "In future, never let any musical sound come out of your mouth unless it has first passed through your mind."

After the preliminary practising of scales and phrases, he looked through a pile of music and selected a song. He sat on the piano stool and looked up at her. "There's something wrong today. We're not in tune, Carina. Perhaps we need a more positive approach. You know this song well, I believe?"

She stood beside him. "*Songs my mother taught me.* Yes, very well."

He played the introductory bars and she began to sing, but it sounded all wrong. She had no guitar, her hands were empty and she groped, first with her hands, then with her voice.

He stopped playing and there was silence. "I'm sorry, Mr. de Verrier," her voice was tearful, "but it's no good. You're making me sing in a way I find impossible. I can't do it. I don't want to do it. You're pushing me into it against my will."

He leaned forward, resting his elbows on the keys, and there was a great clash of discordant notes. He covered his face with his hands. He seemed to be fighting for control, for patience and for the right words.

"Sit down, Carina." She obeyed. He swivelled round and sat astride the piano stool, folding his arms. "Let's get this clear. You are *not* giving up. *I* am not giving up. Where singing is concerned, you have great potential — there is no doubt in my mind about that. Whether that potential develops and comes into its own depends upon the effort both you and I put into it. I want your co-operation. We must work together as a team. You understand?"

"It's no good," she whispered. "You and I are on two different planes, and two planes never meet, any more than two straight lines do."

His eyes narrowed. "Would you kindly explain that statement?"

"Don't you know what I mean?" she asked desperately. "Not only are we incompatible as people, we see the whole subject of singing from two entirely different points of view." She burst out, "Until you came along and started dissecting my voice and trying to put it together again in an entirely different form, I thought I could sing. So did a lot

75

of other people."

"So you thought you could sing?" He went to the door. "Come to my room." She followed him and he unlocked his door, went to his desk and took out the portable cassette recorder she had seen before. "On this is the recording of that performance you gave to the old people's club."

She said defensively, "At the time you praised it."

"I seem to remember I simply called it 'a good performance.' Which it was. I didn't praise your singing. Listen." He played back the recording he had made. It was there again, that pensive, haunting voice, moving the listener to compassion and at times almost to tears.

"What's wrong with that?" she asked belligerently.

"You want me to tell you? All right, but I'm warning you, it will hurt." He counted on his fingers. "You were breathing incorrectly, you were pitching your voice wrongly, your vowels were flat and inhibited instead of full and rounded. Your voice was coming from your throat," he touched it, "instead of from here," his cupped hands fitted round her ribs, "your diaphragm." His touch set her heart pounding, and she almost panicked, wanting to twist away. But with fierce self-control she held still.

"So I was terrible that night." Her lips compressed, her uncertainty increased. He had been right, his criticism did hurt. "So I'm hopeless as a singer."

He softened his voice. "You're only saying that to get me to deny it. Well, I will. You have a wonderful instrument there, Carina. Learn to respect it. Don't ruin it by misusing it, by singing in the wrong way."

He was still holding her and she brought her hand up between them, fiddling with the ring on her finger, looking at it, but not taking in the way it sparkled as the sunlight caught its many facets.

"One day, Carina," he said gently, "you will have to give up these performances to old people's clubs. You will have to give up your guitar. For good. Very soon, now." She was silent and her head was down. He pulled her closer. "I can't

76

let your voice go on living a 'double life' indefinitely. You will have to make your choice. The old way or the new way – my way."

The tears came silently, running down her cheeks, but she pretended they were not there. "It's no good. I can't give up my guitar." Now the tears had invaded her voice. "It would mean giving up my friends. I couldn't sit amongst them in the den listening to them playing and singing, without being able to join in. It would mean giving up singing to the old people, and to your grandfather. And you know how he loves hearing me sing." She shook her head. "It's no use. I can't do it."

He felt in his pocket for his handkerchief and pushed it into her hand. He put his arm across her shoulders but did not attempt to stop her crying. She had come to a time of decision, the parting of the ways. He seemed to guess how much it was hurting her and that in speaking of it as she was meant in itself that she was facing the renunciation of all she cherished so much. But it obviously had not occurred to him to doubt in which direction her final choice would lie.

The door was pushed open and a head came round it, with mousey hair and a pale lifeless face which now creased into a smile. "So you're here, Marcus. I thought you'd be teaching."

He smiled back. "Believe it or not, Faith, I am."

"Sorry to interrupt," she said. "I just thought I'd remind you of our date this evening."

"Oh, yes, the recital."

"You hadn't really forgotten, Marcus, had you?" The voice was wheedling, the smile turning feeble like a flickering candle flame. She turned a poisonous stare at the girl around whose shoulders Marcus's arm was still resting.

"Forget it, Faith? How could I?"

The smile burned brighter as though a draught had fanned it. "Meet you at seven, you said, Marcus." He nodded and she withdrew reluctantly, after a pause in

77

which she seemed to be waiting for that arm to be removed from those bent shoulders.

Carina had by now recovered a little, and she returned the handkerchief. As Marcus released her, she wondered what she must look like. Her face was burning, her forehead moist, her hair damp here and there where it had touched the tears on her cheeks. "I'm sorry, Mr. de Verrier."

He went to the piano, and stood with his fingers trailing the keys. "I'm used to it, Carina. It's the tension, plus the effort. Not to mention artistic temperament. Girl students often break down and cry all over me."

So he was reducing her to the level of all the others. Why shouldn't he? What was she to him that he should make an exception of her?

At the door she turned. "Mr. de Verrier?" He looked at her, raising his eyebrows in a kindly way. "There's another walk tomorrow. The others have been asking when you're coming with us again." Still standing, he ran his fingers over the keys, his foot depressing the soft pedal. "We're meeting in the usual place." He stopped playing. "Can I — can I tell them you'll be coming?"

He pushed his hands into his pockets and sighed. "You never know, Carina, you never know." He smiled and his face came alive. "If I feel energetic enough, I might well join you. And," she turned back, "thanks for asking me."

That evening, knowing Marcus would be out, Carina drove to Ernest de Verrier's. She had to talk to someone. She was still undecided, although she had thought it over again and again. But like someone lost in a forest, she had come back every time to the same place.

She unburdened herself to Ernest, and as she talked the decision she was going to make became clear. "I don't think I can do what he's asking, Mr. de Verrier. It would mean giving up so much, like giving up part of my life. I'd lose my friends, I'd lose you —"

"Never me, lass. You could still come here."

"But I'd never be able to sing to you in the old way. It

78

would mean taking a pleasure away from you, too." I'm piling on the agony, she thought, to make him see it my way, to make him come over to my side, to reassure me I'm taking the right decision.

"Never mind me, Carrie. It's your future in the balance, your career."

'Her career.' He was, without knowing it, prodding at her conscience with a sharp stick. A career, something to aim at, a reason for living, instead of just existing in a vacuum. But her guitar, her friends ... She couldn't do it.

A car drew up in the driveway. She stared at Ernest, her eyes wide with fright. "Marcus? So early?"

"He never stays out late, lass, no matter who he's with."

"I must go. You don't mind, Mr. de Verrier?"

"Stay a while, Carrie," he pleaded, but she was inching out of the door. "Well, if you must go, you must."

She met Marcus in the hall and, averting her head, rushed past him as though he were giving off poisonous fumes.

By the frown on his face he seemed to be in a bad humour and her speedy exit at the sight of him must have exacerbated it. His arm shot out and stopped her, pulling her into the living-room. "Where the devil are you going in such a hurry just because I've come home? Did you think I'd got designs on your chastity?"

Ernest winced. A temperate, kindly man, he had not been able to accustom himself to the bluntness of the younger generation in matters which were, to him, sacred and strictly private and which should, in his opinion, remain so.

"Don't be silly," she said, clawing unsuccessfully at the fingers which gripped her wrist, "I'm going home, that's all."

"If that were really all, I'd let you go. But something deep inside me tells me it's not all." Again Carina tried to break away, but he held her still. "There's an atmosphere in here which is so thick if I had a knife I could slice into it. I know what you've been doing. You've been talking things over with my grandfather. Not with me, of course, who could advise you professionally, but with someone paternal – or perhaps I should say grand-paternal – whom you can twist round your little finger like a length of wool."

"I think you frighten her, Marcus," Ernest said placatingly.

"You must be joking! This girl, with her fortune, afraid of a man with, by comparison, hardly a penny to his name?"

"It's true, lad. The way she's been talking this evening . ."

"What about?" his grandson barked.

"All right, all right. She always brings her troubles to me. No one else listens to her, do they, Carrie?"

Marcus turned to Carina. "You've got parents. What about them?" She shook her head. "With your money," he said viciously, "you could afford to *pay* someone to listen to your outpourings."

Tears sprang to her eyes, and not only because his fingers had settled even more firmly round her wrist.

Ernest flinched at his grandson's callousness. "You're asking her to do something she can't face."

There was an icy silence. "Is this true, Carina? Is that what you have decided?"

"Yes," she whispered. "Please try to understand."

But he flung her wrist away and with it her appeal for clemency.

"Right, now I know just where I stand. I wash my hands of you. From this moment on, Carina Ascott can go to hell!"

He slammed out of the room.

Carina covered her face and sank on to the stool. Ernest sighed. He was shaking a little. "If only Marcus knew the truth," he said, "if only you would tell him . . ."

"What would be the use, Mr. de Verrier?" she whispered

behind her hands. "He hates me so much, even if he did know, it wouldn't make any difference."

"You may be right, lass," Ernest murmured, nodding sadly, "you may well be right."

Marcus did not join them on the walk. Until the last minute Carina hoped he might. They even delayed their departure in case he was late.

It was autumn. The day was grey, the leaves, bronzed like someone who had spent the summer in the tropics, clung valiantly to the branches, defying the winds to wrench them from their perch. Hands in her pockets, Carina pushed her feet into the crunching leaf-mould lying thick on the path, listening to the chatter and laughter around her.

Seth walked beside her until he grew tired of her moping silence, then he dropped behind and she walked alone. They had tea in the café amongst the trees and returned to Carina's den in the grounds of her home.

They played and sang, but Carina held back until they asked her what was wrong.

"Come on, Carina," Seth urged, "let's do our new one, *The Conscience of the world.*" He moved to sit beside her and started to play. She opened her mouth to sing, found herself wondering which of her two voices to use, and in those few seconds of indecision, her fate was decided.

She chose the old voice, but knew instinctively that it would be for the last time. It felt wrong, it sounded wrong. As she listened to herself, she listened not with her own ears, but with Marcus's, criticising her own breathing, her vowel sounds, the pitch of her voice.

At the end, Seth asked, "What's the matter?"

So he had noticed. Had the others? Judging by their faces, they had. "Sorry, Seth, not in the mood. Get someone else to sing for you. Olwen?"

The two girls changed places, and as Carina listened to Olwen's singing, she found herself criticising that, too. She took a back seat for the rest of the afternoon, retreating into herself, listening, hearing the others' pleasure, envying them their uncomplicated lives, their freedom to sing as they chose. She remembered, like a dying man, the past happiness she had shared with them, but even as she mourned its passing, she felt inside her the birth pangs of the future – her future, pushing itself into the world like a baby being born, separating itself, yet still part of her, the person she was going to become.

Although Marcus was absent, she felt he was there, and she knew that in coming at last to her decision, it had been his influence which had made her decide, his magnetism – which she had felt even when they had first met – which she had been unable to resist, and which in the last analysis had made her choice inevitable.

CHAPTER FIVE

CARINA did not enjoy her piano lessons. She did not like Faith Ringstead. She sat in the practice room waiting for the woman to appear, and stared out of the window at the houses across the road.

Marcus had been conspicuous by his absence in the past few days. Even when she had caught a glimpse of him he was always at the other end of the corridor. Miss Ringstead came in, her pale face wreathed in self-satisfied smiles. What did Marcus see in her? Carina wondered. Was it that she was the exact antithesis of the rich girl he was once engaged to? Was it that, if matters were to progress far enough between them, this woman would be so unattractive to any other man she could not possibly let Marcus down as his ex-fiancée had done?

"I've just come," Miss Ringstead said, "from Mar — I mean, Mr. de Verrier. He's furious with you. He said you're giving up singing. He told me to work you till you drop. He said you've got to be made to be good at something, otherwise you might as well give up."

The lesson which followed was disastrous. Carina did her best, which in the circumstances was not very good, but her mind was elsewhere, arguing with Marcus, fighting for her right to remain a student in the school of music.

Miss Ringstead kept shifting her off the piano stool and showing her how it should be done. The woman's playing was mechanical and cold, as unmoving and passionless as the player herself, the performance of someone who had never known what it was to give herself in any way, either in love or in life itself.

Carina copied exactly the teacher's own style because she simply could not be bothered to do otherwise. But Miss Ringstead, who could not hear herself, tore the performance to pieces. Carina let the criticism roll off her. She simply did not care. After the lesson she would go and see Marcus. The sooner matters were straightened out between them the better.

Miss Ringstead let her go with a series of tuts and a disgusted toss of the head. "I'll have to tell Mr. de Verrier," she said, "how badly you're doing."

Carina raced along the corridor to Marcus's room. As she raised her hand to knock, she heard voices inside. There was someone with him. Later she tried again, but the room was empty.

There was a letter from Avery waiting for her at home. He missed her, he said, more and more as the days went by. Why didn't she write to him? And had she changed his ring to her left hand yet? If not, he would do it for her at Christmas when he hoped to fly home for a short holiday. Her father, he said, had suggested it, and that if they liked they could have an engagement party then. Carina folded the letter away. As far as she was concerned, there would be no engagement to celebrate.

Later, Carina drove to Ernest's house. As she pushed open the front door, she saw Marcus sprinting up the stairs.

"Mr. de Verrier?" she called, but his door slammed shut. So he was getting out of the way before she arrived. He must have seen her car draw up. It was a calculated rebuff.

Ernest's face was flushed when she went in. Her concern was immediate and urgent. "Something wrong, Mr. de Verrier?"

"Just a bit of an argument with my grandson, lass. Trying to make him see reason about – well, some things is like

84

King Canute trying to hold back the sea. You just get no-where."

Carina sat on the footstool, her guitar on her lap. She still could not bring herself to leave it behind. "It wasn't about – me, was it, Mr. de Verrier?" Ernest seemed to be pretending to be deaf. It was one of his tricks. It had often got him out of awkward situations, he said. "I wanted to see Marcus," she went on, "but it's obvious he doesn't want to see me."

Ernest's deafness cleared remarkably quickly. "Go on up, Carrie. He'll be glad to see you."

They looked at each other and laughed, Ernest chestily, Carina heartily. "If that isn't the biggest falsehood of all time!" she said.

She put her guitar aside. She couldn't take that upstairs. No sense in baiting the lion in his den as well as braving him. It needed all her courage to climb the stairs and tap on his door. He did not answer. He must have guessed who it was. His grandfather would hardly have tapped as gently as that – he would probably have used his voice to gain entry.

She knocked again and this time the door opened. "Yes?" The voice was as cold as the eyes.

"May I – may I have a word with you?"

He did not move. In the half-light on the landing he saw the uncertain but entirely predictable frown.

"*Please*, Marcus," softly.

He did not give an inch. Instead he smiled cynically. "Trying to get round me by wheedling your way in? Using the pleading little-girl technique to get my sympathy?" He saw the tightly clasped hands, the appeal in those disturbing eyes and moved aside to let her in.

"I fail to see," he said to her back as she looked round the room taking her bearings, "what there is for us to talk about."

She faced him, but his implacable face gave her no encouragement. "Miss Ringstead said you were furious with me because I was giving up singing. You also told her," her

85

voice faltered, "to work me till I dropped."

"I did. What of it? Someone has to make you learn the hard way."

"I'd like to talk to you about – well, about everything." He made no response. The tension inside her had reached an unbearable limit, and it was as much as she could do to stop herself from shaking.

His eyes moved from her face and strayed over her low-cut ribbed sweater and tightly fitting trousers. She had never seen such an expression in his eyes before and her colour deepened. With deliberation he moved away as if he preferred a greater distance between them.

Carina interpreted his action as indicating that she repelled him. Her hand went to her throat as though there was a rope round it, choking her. He saw the ring, flashing as it moved. The sight of it must have plunged him back into the past, because his lips tightened.

"Please sit down," he said with a politeness that chilled. She obeyed gladly. He remained standing. She had not expected this cold formality and did not know how to cope with it.

It was easier to pretend he was not standing a few yards away, so she said to the window, "I've changed my mind. I'm – I'm not giving up singing." Then she did look at him, but there was no sign of the pleasure she had anticipated.

Instead he said tonelessly, "The prerogative of your kind, of course. What is there to stop you changing your mind back?"

Her eyes opened, her colour flared. "So you don't take me seriously?" He gazed back at her, unmoved. "I wish I could tell you what a struggle I had in coming to my decision, what it cost me to give up my friends, my – my guitar . . ." She choked, "What's the use of talking to you? You wrote me off as useless the day you met me." She ran to the door.

But he was there before her and removing her hand from

86

the door handle. He had come to life at last.

"You and I, my dear Carina," he led her back to the chair, "have a great deal of talking to do." He stood over her, legs apart, hands in pockets. "Now, tell me what that little speech of yours meant. Have you, after all, decided on a career of singing? And you're putting yourself in my hands?"

"Yes, Marcus."

"You realise it will be hard work, sheer unadulterated slog – there's no other word for it – and even sheer hell at times?"

"Yes, Marcus."

"You will have to practise, practise and practise again. You'll have to envelop yourself in music, drown in it in fact, rarely coming up for air. You know we shall have to work as a team, you and I? And that you'll have to put your trust in me as a teacher, an adviser and as a man? Will you be able to do that, Carina?"

She whispered again, "Yes, Marcus."

Now there was a light in his eyes, of anticipation and of triumph, as though she had given him some wonderful gift. And yet it was she who would be the recipient of his knowledge, of his patience and his teaching. She would be the beneficiary, not the other way round. If one day she succeeded in her chosen career, it would be she who would gain the rewards, not he.

"I didn't realise until now," she said, "how incredibly unselfish a teacher is. I shall be getting the benefit of your knowledge. You'll get nothing out of it."

He seemed so pleased she could not believe it. It was almost as though he liked her. But that, she knew, was an illusion.

"You're wrong, Carina. As your teacher I shall share with you the pleasure of your successes. Believe me, it will mean as much to me as it will to you. Teachers are always delighted when their pupils succeed."

"You're so confident that I will."

"I have every faith in you." She frowned and he asked, "Why the uncertainty, Carina?"

"It's as well you have confidence in me, Marcus. I have none in myself!"

Her self-doubt seemed to touch his compassion at last, throwing him momentarily off guard. He stretched out his hand to cover hers, but she drew back at once. His eyes flickered – it could have been with anger – and for a moment the antipathy he felt for all she represented flared in his eyes, but it passed. She supposed he was thinking that if she could not even stand his touch, it was all the better. He obviously wanted no involvement with any woman, and certainly not with any girl called Carina Ascott.

They joined Ernest in the living-room and made plans, charting her course and discussing in which direction her future lay.

After the truce, as Carina liked to think of it, the singing lessons became a delight. Marcus was charm itself, drawing from her the best she had to give.

Faith Ringstead had spoken so badly of Carina's progress with the piano, Marcus even took over those lessons, too. It was essential, he said, for her to do well in another subject besides that of singing, otherwise she would not qualify to pass on to a London school of music, and that, he said, would be disastrous to her career.

Marcus's friendship with Faith Ringstead continued. To the outsider, it appeared to be purely platonic, but Carina told herself miserably, one could not judge by outward appearances. It would not do for either of them to display any emotion towards each other while at work. But afterwards, when they were out together in the evenings, only they knew what happened between them. After all, Carina tortured herself with the thought, Faith lived alone in a furnished flat ...

In his relationship with Carina, also, Marcus was most meticulous during their lessons together; it was on a strict teacher-student basis, in spite of her friendship with his

88

grandfather and her frequent visits to the house Marcus shared with him.

A concert had been planned for presentation shortly before the end of the autumn term. Both first- and second-year students would be taking part and Marcus was grooming Carina to appear.

He had taught her to have a picture in her mind as she sang, and had told her to try to pass that picture on to the audience.

"You must bridge the space between yourself and your listeners with your mind," he said, "then with your voice, in that order. You must experience what you are singing, because singing is a pouring out of your own feelings."

One afternoon Marcus took her through the songs she would be singing at the concert. First came a group of songs by Schubert, followed by the song she had chosen herself, one which she loved and which she had sung in the past to the old people. It was *Ich Liebe Dich* by Grieg.

As he played the first bars, she closed her eyes and a picture flashed into her mind. Panicking, she opened them, but the picture was still there. She began to sing, in German as Marcus had instructed, and she could not take her eyes from his face. Her heart was in her voice, her whole body vibrating with the knowledge that had come to her, and which had flooded her mind with longing – and an endless sadness. *Ich Liebe Dich*, she sang, *I love thee*, and she knew it was a love that would never be returned.

He played the accompaniment with his usual sensitivity. Now and then he lifted his eyes and looked into hers. When the song was over there was a deep silence.

He asked, softly, gently, "Were you singing to me?" She could not bring herself to answer his question. "I quite understand, Carina. Many students fall in love with their teachers. It's nothing unusual. An occupational hazard, in fact. But I prefer to call it infatuation, which will pass with time." His fingers moved over the keys and a quiet, haunting piece of music filled the room. "In all the circum-

89

stances, it must, mustn't it? It simply would not work," as though he had given the matter some thought and arrived at that inescapable conclusion. He looked at her hand, her right hand. "You have a young man of your own." He paused, perhaps waiting for a denial, but none came.

"Sing the song again, Carina, this time having a picture in your mind of your boy-friend, not of me."

She heard the introduction, opened her mouth and tried to obey him, but she could not overcome the lump in her throat.

He stopped, telling her sharply to pull herself together. "What is it you want?" he snapped, angry now with her and, it seemed, with himself too, for losing control, "a declaration of love from me, too? I'm sorry, it's just not on."

"Do you have to be so brutal?" she asked thickly.

Their eyes held, his containing no expression, not even of anger. Any emotion, Carina thought miserably, would have been better than that repelling blankness.

It was useless to continue the lesson. The mood had gone, her feelings were in a turmoil, like a city street after a bomb had exploded. She asked, her voice high and strained, "May I go, Mr. de Verrier?"

He nodded, taking the music from the stand and closing the piano.

Now it was almost winter. The trees in the forest were bare, their branches black and angular against the grey November sky. Not a hint of a breeze stirred the bushes as the group waited on the edge of the forest, delaying the start of the walk to make sure no latecomers were left behind.

Carina was talking to Seth when a car door slammed and someone called her name. She looked round. "Marcus!" It was impossible to hide her pleasure, and she almost ran to him.

The others greeted him with a delight which nearly

equalled hers. They surrounded him and she was cut off. As they walked along the familiar paths, Carina trailed behind. She had given up long ago trying to get near him. It was not difficult for her to take a back seat; she had been conditioned to it by experience, by the birth of Justine. Now she accepted it as her lot.

It was enough, she told herself, that he was there among them, that he had felt the urge to come. After what he had said at the singing lesson yesterday, she did not fool herself that she had been the motivating force behind his action.

She inhaled the heavy autumnal scents, the smell of the bracken, the misty dampness in the air. It was not until they had nearly reached the tea place that Marcus seemed to remember her. He held back, letting the others pass him and went to her side, smiling down at her.

"You don't exactly go out of your way to make your presence felt, do you, Carina? Why are you always so withdrawn?"

"I didn't know I was." Her eyes were alive and bright because he had come to her.

"One can never tell what you're thinking."

He was rooting, like a police dog, too near the secret places in her mind. "Thanks," she said, putting him off the scent, "for assuming that I do think!" She stopped and gazed up into his eyes. "You know what I'm thinking now?"

He gazed back at her, as if caught by some evidence which would lead him to the vital clue. "Tell me."

She laughed. "That I'm hungry and want my tea!"

He reached down and gave her a single playful spank. She laughed again and followed the others into the café. Seth sat beside her at the long wooden table where their tea was served. Marcus was at the other end. Afterwards, when they left the café, Seth's arm went round Carina's shoulders and she did not object. They walked this way for some time, and she caught Marcus's speculative eyes on them once or twice.

"We miss you," Seth said. "Especially me. No one to write the lyrics to my songs, no one to sing them as I like them sung."

"Blame Marcus," Carina said, looking at Marcus's broad back a few yards in front. "He inveigled me away from folk music, from the music of real people. Now I only perform the conventional stuff which is sung in an artificial atmosphere on a stage to people who come prepared to listen but not join in. Most of them anyway only go to a concert for the look of the thing, and not for the love of the music."

Marcus stopped in his tracks and turned, walking back the few yards which separated them. "Was that," he asked tersely, "meant sincerely, or merely to provoke?"

He was blocking the path, so Carina sidestepped and moved to pass him, but he caught her arm and swung her back to face him. Seth joined the others.

She dislodged his hand which was beginning to hurt, but she did not reply.

"Explain yourself," he insisted. "I'm not letting you go until you do. If it was genuine, it's of vital importance that we talk this out."

"It was genuine," she said, a little sullenly.

His manner softened and they walked on. "What is troubling you, Carina?"

"It's just that –" she groped for the right words, "that the sort of music I'm having to sing these days has no – no message, no application to the problems of the day, in fact it doesn't belong to the present day at all." She stopped, expecting him to remonstrate, but he said nothing. He was staring at the dead leaves underfoot, scuffed up by the others in front of them. She went on, "I won't be able to make contact as I used to. I won't be able to 'touch' the people down in the auditorium as I used to 'touch' the old people who listened to me in those halls." She looked up at him. "They'll be self-conscious, dressed in their best, out of my reach. The people I used to sing to were human and not afraid to show it. They gave me their warmth and showed their pleasure, and their tears, without being embarrassed about it." She paused for breath. "That's what is worrying me, Marcus." There was a question in her voice, like a child wanting an adult's reassurance that all its fears were groundless.

"It really is worrying you, Carina?" He smiled down at her. "I'm glad. It means you're beginning to care at last, which pleases me. But you're wrong, quite wrong. I'll tell you something. There's a quality in your voice which, however you sing and whatever you sing, is infinitely moving and which, as my grandfather says, 'gets right down and touches them'. You'll be giving joy to people in a different way. You will be singing in such a manner that you'll be conveying to the audience your very thoughts, making them enjoy what you enjoy and feel what you are feeling." He caught her hand and pressed it. "Does that make you any happier?"

His fingers entwined with hers and she could only nod. "And not only will you charm them with your voice," he went on, "but with your looks. You're attractive, with an," he seemed lost for the right word, "an appealing sort of beauty about you. I hope," he lifted her right hand and looked at the ring, "the man you're going to marry appreciates you." He led her over a wooden plank which spanned a stream. "Do your parents approve of him, Carina?"

"Who?" she asked. "Avery? Approve of him? They want me to marry him so much they're practically pushing him into my arms with a house and a fortune thrown in as a special offer!"

He laughed, but his amusement was short-lived. "That's half the battle, take it from me." Now he sounded cynical. "Parental approval is a commodity no young couple should even hold hands without."

She tried to pull her fingers away. "Then we'd better disentangle, hadn't we?"

"My word," he said in mock alarm, "you're right." And, to her chagrin, they did.

The crowd was waiting for them at the edge of the forest. "Coming with us, Marcus?" Olwen asked.

Marcus looked at Carina. "What goes on? I thought we all retired to your den?"

"Not any more," Seth told him. "Carina couldn't join in and it was agony for her having to listen to us, so we've taken pity on her and go round to each other's houses instead."

Carina made her face blank. "You can go with them, Marcus. I don't mind." She crossed the road and made for the den. Marcus shouted, "Wait for me," said his goodbyes to the others and caught her up. "I know it's impolite for a guest to invite himself . . ."

"Sorry, Marcus, do come in."

He made straight for the harpsichord, asked, "Do you mind?" and sat at the keyboard with his back to her.

While he played, she picked up her guitar which was propped against a wall, sat on a stool and fingered the strings, bending her head and "listening" as if she were really playing. The door was standing open and a chill breeze was blowing in. Oblivious to it, she watched the darkness descending over the gardens, the low-lying clouds shrouding the lily pond with a blanket of reflected grey, and veiling the stone figure which rose from the centre of the pool.

The music had stopped and Marcus was standing over her, cutting off the view. It was almost dark in the den. She asked, "What were you playing?"

"Bach." He looked at her guitar on which she was still miming a tune, and laughed. "You look so pathetic doing that." He tilted her face and searched her troubled eyes. "Why so melancholy, Carina, when you have the world to conquer? One day people will flock to hear you and you'll be mesmerising them as you mesmerise – people who know you now." He lifted her left hand away from the guitar and ran his thumb over the tips of her fingers. "The hard skin – it's nearly gone." She took her hand from his.

94

"Yes." Her voice was bitter. "You've cured me of my 'addiction' as you once called it. You've almost weaned me away from my guitar. You should be proud of your achievement."

He removed the guitar from her, putting it against a chair, and pulled her up, resting his hands on her shoulders and looking into her eyes which glowed in the near darkness.

"Will you ever forgive me for my selfishness?" he asked softly. "Layer by layer I've stripped you of the things you loved – your folk music, your singing, your guitar, your friends. Why did you let me?"

She gazed up at him, straining, without success, to see his expression. Because, she wanted to say, of the power you've had over me from the start. I felt it the first day we met. I feel it now. I love your grandfather. I love you. There must be something about the de Verrier family.

"There must be something about you," she said with a smile.

He laughed – was there an exultant sound in his laughter? – and picked up the guitar. He sat on a stool beside her and played a few notes. "If I asked you to sing to me now, would you?"

Her head shot round. "Are you testing me?"

"Perhaps. What shall it be, Carina? *Plaisir d'Amour?* A pause. *"Ich Liebe Dich?"*

A longer pause. "Now you're tormenting me." He played the taunting, haunting accompaniment to *Ich Liebe Dich*, and she stirred, unable to bear it. By choosing that particular song, he was mocking her. "I couldn't sing as I used to any more," she flung at him, "even if I were paid a fortune to do so. You've put all that beyond my reach."

She went to the door. Only good manners prevented her from running away and leaving him, a guest, alone. He put aside the guitar and was after her swiftly. He turned her round. "Carina? Will you believe me when I say I'm sorry?"

His hands went to her waist and although she drew herself in because of the torment of his touch, he did not let her go. There was a minimum of light coming in through the door and it turned them both into shadows. His eyes, narrowing in an effort to see, dwelt on her mouth. The bright beauty in the darkness was a magnet and it could not be resisted.

His lips came upon hers and held with a certainty which betrayed his confidence that she would receive his kiss with pleasure and that he would not be repulsed. His arms slipped round her and tightened. The kiss went on, but although her pulses leapt at the feel of him, and her body began to yield to his persuasive hands, there was no joy inside her, only pain.

With a violence that surprised even herself, she twisted out of his arms. "What are you doing," she cried, "humouring me? Kissing it better? Save yourself the bother. And isn't it dangerous to encourage me? It's only infatuation, remember. It will pass, you said so yourself."

He shrugged and his arms went slackly to his sides. He propped himself against the doorway and stared out, but there was little enough to see because it was pitch dark now.

Whatever had flared between them had blazed for a few fiery seconds and burnt itself out.

"Marcus?" into the deep silence.

"Yes?"

"Would you like to come into the house?"

"Why?"

"The piano, Marcus – I thought you might like to play it." As if offering a child a sweet as a bribe to take some medicine, she added, "It makes a beautiful sound." There was no response. "My parents are out."

"So I wouldn't have to declare my intentions. Thank God for that!"

"Forget it." There were tears in her voice.

"I'm sorry, Carina, I was just reminiscing. The past

keeps catching up with me. It's haunting me these days like a fiendish ghost." He straightened. "I should very much like to go into your house and play your piano."

She led the way through the garden, across the patio and into the kitchen. "I hope you don't mind going in the back way," she said.

The housekeeper, Mrs. Jenner, was preparing the evening meal. She smiled, nodded, inspected Marcus in detail, raised her eyebrows at what she saw and carried on with her work.

Carina led the way across the blue-carpeted hall into the main drawing-room, switching on all the lights as she entered. Marcus stopped at the door to take in the splendour of his companion's background.

The room was large enough to fit in his grandfather's living-room three times over. There were paintings on the walls of nineteenth-century French painters – Cézanne, Millet, Pissaro. There were portraits of the family. He studied them.

Mother, small, fair, elegantly smiling; father, just a little pompous, sandy hair receding; a young girl, also fair, petite, beautiful. Carina, black-haired, brown-eyed, shapely, in her eyes the look of the rebel, on her face a look of dissociation from the whole project.

"Where, for heaven's sake," he asked, "is the similarity, the family likeness? It's there in your sister – Justine, isn't it? – but you?"

He turned, puzzled, and caught her looking at him with the expression of someone who had hidden something away and thought it was in imminent danger of being uncovered.

"I must," she said with a tight, nervous smile, "be a throwback."

"You must, indeed. The odd one out."

How that hurt. But then the truth often did.

"The piano, Marcus."

He strolled towards it. The polished rosewood shone, the ivory gleamed. "May I?" He sat on the piano stool, lifted his hands, paused as if thinking what to play and went softly, movingly, into the Moonlight Sonata. He played for a long time as if he could not bring himself to stop. But at last his hands were still.

"That," he murmured, "was an experience." He swivelled round to look up at her as she moved to his side. "And you say this piano is yours?"

"Mine."

"So when you marry, you take it with you?" She nodded. "My word," he grinned, "shall I take advantage of this so-called infatuation you're alleged to have for me, sweep you off your feet and marry you tomorrow? Then the piano would be mine, too." He stood and faced her, his hand groping for hers, but she backed away. He was still smiling. "It's almost worth the sacrifice."

"Sacrifice? Of what?"

"My freedom."

"Then keep your freedom. The deal's off. I should almost certainly live up to my reputation and be awkward. I would probably lock the piano and hide the key!"

He sighed exaggeratedly. "Then I'm afraid I must withdraw my proposal."

"I wasn't aware that you had made one. Marcus, would you —" that doubtful look again, "would you like to come upstairs and see my stereo equipment?"

He laughed. "That sounds like a proposal of a different sort. Now who's doing the encouraging? In the den it was I. Here, it's you." He bowed mockingly. "Lead the way, Carina. Who am I to refuse such a promising invitation?"

She stood still on her way to the door. "Don't be silly, Marcus. I didn't mean —"

"I'm sure you didn't." He grinned, enjoying her confusion. "But in future, be careful how you word an invitation to your bedroom. And," softly, "whom you invite." He looked her over and she flushed. "A girl with your attractions would, in the right circumstances, go to the head of any man, however sober he might normally be, and even if he had renounced women, as I have — except, that is, as a temporary distraction."

"So I'm a 'temporary distraction'?"

"You sound annoyed. Why? Did you want to be anything else?"

She coloured deeply at his taunt and swept up the stairs. The bedroom was large, the décor simple but effective. The curtains, white with pink flowers strewn over them, matched the quilt. There was a ceiling-high built-in wardrobe with sliding doors, one of which was standing open, revealing the multitude of dresses, slacks and evening wear inside.

"You can hardly say," he commented dryly, "that you haven't a 'rag to your back'."

She slid the door shut with a loud bang.

Against the wall was a bureau. "This is an antique," Marcus commented.

"My father bought it for me," she answered carelessly. "Here's the stereo equipment."

He strolled across the room and looked it over with the eye of an expert. "Another gift? From your father?" Again the careless nod. "As with the piano and the harpsichord and everything else, only the best, I see."

She watched at first while he tried it out, then wandered to the dressing-table and picked up the jewellery strewn over it. She put some of the necklaces against her, put them down and pushed them aside as though they were worthless. She thought, if I show him I don't care about these things, he'll see how little they mean to me.

With a thrust of fear she saw in the mirror that he was standing beside her. His reflected eyes were as hard as the diamonds she had treated so casually.

"You," he said softly, "are as careless of your possessions as everyone else in this world who has a surfeit of money. You can deny it as much as you like, but my God, as Seth says, it would take a millionaire to keep up with your tastes and requirements!"

So her little ruse had misfired, had provoked the opposite reaction to the one she had anticipated. She was thinking hopelessly, I'd leave it all behind tomorrow if I had the chance. But if she had said those words aloud, he would have misinterpreted them, too.

He stood behind her and with his arms encircling her waist pulled her back to rest against him. Wherever he touched her, her body throbbed and she wished desperately that he would stop tantalising her and leave her alone. He was so much taller than she was she had to lift her eyes to look at his reflecting back at her. "Don't you realise," he shook her a little, "what a fortunate young woman you are?"

"Am I fortunate?"

He saw only her smile and did not notice the seriousness of her tone. He tutted and turned his head from side to side as if he had given her up. He swivelled her round to face him. "Ungrateful little minx, aren't you?"

She gazed up at him, and he lifted a finger to try to smooth away the frown. She wondered, has he never seen presents of conscience before, compensatory gifts to take the place of the love my parents diverted from me to their beloved Justine, their real daughter, when she was born?

A car swept into the semi-circular drive at the front of the house. She tensed and stared at Marcus. "My parents are back."

He frowned, letting her go. "What are you afraid of? Is it such a calamity?"

He followed her along the landing and down the stairs. As they reached the hall, Phyllis and Lloyd came in. With surprise, then suspicion, and even, oddly, with a trace of apprehension, they looked at the strange young man at Carina's side. Then they looked at her, noting her high colour and the way she was gazing up at him.

Carina was thinking, "Why is he looking at them like that, as if he had seen them somewhere before?" What will he think of them? she wondered. Why did they have to arrive at that moment? Why couldn't Marcus have gone before they came home? She knew what he would think of them. It was there in his eyes. She knew what he would think of her, now. Reluctantly she made the introductions.

Phyllis and Lloyd moved together as if scenting danger and finding safety in numbers. It was as if they had made an unspoken agreement to repel this mysterious intruder at all costs. On cue came the condescension, the lady-of-the-manor smile, and because this young man seemed so much more dangerous than all Carina's other male acquaintances, the superciliousness of Phyllis's manner increased in proportion to the threat he posed to their peace of mind.

"How do you do, Mr. – er – de Verrier? You're one of our daughter's – er – friends, a new one? She has so many, you know, I really can't keep count!"

"Marcus is head of the school of music, Mother."

"*Is* he, dear?" Her tone was carefully calculated to disparage the position.

"I teach your daughter singing, Mrs. Ascott."

At the sound of Marcus's voice, pleasant, controlled, educated, both parents' eyebrows lifted, and they exchanged meaningful glances, as if mutely agreeing to put on the pressure.

"A teacher, eh?" Lloyd's hearty laughter did nothing to hide the contempt in his eyes. "Wasn't it Bernard Shaw who said, 'Those who can, do, those who can't, teach'? Oh, well, I suppose someone's got to educate the kids, even if it is people who have failed in their own subject."

"A teacher," Phyllis contributed flatly, "oh."

"He's really a musician, Mother," Carina said, with desperate patience. How much worse can this get? she wondered hopelessly. Her hand brushed Marcus's and she found to her dismay that it was clenched into a fist.

"A *musician*?" Now there was a hint of horror in the tone.

Marcus looked at his watch. "I must go, Carina." He raised his eyebrows in his most autocratic manner and said in clipped tones to Phyllis and Lloyd, "Will you excuse me, please?"

"But of course, Mr. – er – de –" Phyllis had lost the name.

"Verri-ay," finished Lloyd, with the smile of a conjurer taking a rabbit from a hat.

"No, Mr. Ascott," Marcus corrected, his tone studiedly patient, "Verri-er, plain, simple Verri-*er*. Nothing fancy. And incidentally, the 'de' in front of it is pure chance," his eyes glinted, "probably the result of a questionable act on the part of some distant female ancestor of mine with a member of the French nobility."

He waited a moment for his shock tactics to take effect, then, satisfied at having taken revenge for their hostility and contempt, he swept out into the darkness.

"I'll show you to your car, Marcus," Carina called frantically. "It's round the back. You might get lost."

He did not wait for her, so she ran after him. "Marcus, I –"

He stood beside his car, feeling in his pockets for the keys. "Teacher," he muttered savagely, "in their eyes a species caught and crystallised for all time by Dickens, living in poverty and using a quill pen. 'Musician' equals 'artist' equals 'garret', which brings you back to poverty."

He looked at the girl at his side and said with bitterness, "Rebellious daughter opposes parents' wishes in marrying said pauper. Defies them till the last, when she suddenly sees the 'light', the miseries of marrying out of her social and financial class. Breaks off engagement, throws the ring in your face, marries rich boy-friend and lives opulently ever after."

"But, Marcus, please –"

He wrenched her hand away from the car door and unlocked it. "I've seen it all before. And when you argue and fight to get her back, she insults you by saying, 'We've had lots of fun, haven't we, darling? Don't let's spoil the memory by fighting.' " He made a vicious noise with his throat. He put his hands on her arms and moved her forcibly to one side. "You'd better get out of my way and keep out of it, unless you want to take the brunt of my temper."

"But, Marcus," she whimpered, crying now, "*Marcus!*" She tried to stop him by holding on to the car, but he wound down the window and dragged her hand away from the handle. Then he roared away down the road.

All day Monday Carina tried to see Marcus. She wanted to say she was sorry. She did not quite know on what grounds she owed him an apology, although she felt one was due. But he proved too elusive to find.

She ran him to earth eventually at his grandfather's house. Ernest, it seemed, was upstairs, but Marcus was in the kitchen washing up.

He turned from the sink as she stood in the kitchen doorway and asked her coldly what she wanted. Nothing much, she told him lamely. His grandfather, he replied, was upstairs. "Go into the living-room and wait for him."

But she stayed where she was. She watched him for a few moments, longing to take over from him. Her pity, all her feminine instincts were aroused by the sight of this accomplished, talented man doing such work, and doing it without complaint.

Unable to bear the sight of him working unaided any longer, she took a tea towel and started drying up. She did it warily, expecting a rebuff, but strangely none came.

She said, hesitantly, "Marcus? I'd like to say I'm sorry. About the other evening. About my mother and —"

"For God's sake," he said, "don't apologise for your parents." The way he knew what she was talking about meant that the incident was still clear in his mind, perhaps even that he had been dwelling on it. Her heart sank. He went on, "You were not presenting me to them for their inspection as a possible husband."

She answered with enforced calm, "I introduced you as my singing teacher, remember."

"Oh, yes. So you did!" His tone was ingenuous, then it changed. "I also remember their reaction to the information. I plainly failed to pass their rigid test as a fitting companion for their beloved offspring."

"Which is why I wanted to apologise." He looked up at the quiet tone. "I'm not my parents' keeper, Marcus."

"Agreed. But you are your parents' daughter. That you can't deny."

I could, oh, but I could, she thought. I could tell you the truth here and now. I could say, I'm adopted. But if I did, what difference would it make to your attitude to me? None at all. You would say I've got so conditioned to the world and ways of my adoptive parents that I have inevitably become part of them, having absorbed them irreversibly into my system.

Ernest came down the stairs, each foot feeling for the next tread. Carina went to greet him.

"Hallo, Carina love." He welcomed her with a kiss on the cheek while his grandson leaned against a wall and watched. "It's been a long time since you came to see your old friend, Carrie. I thought you'd forgotten me."

"Never!" Carina laughed.

They went into the living-room and Ernest lowered himself into his favourite chair. Carina hoped Marcus would follow, but was convinced he would go straight upstairs. He did join them, however, and she had to quell the pleasure which made the blood race through her veins. She took her usual place on the footstool.

Ernest went on, "You've been seeing so much of my grandson lately, I thought you'd stopped loving me and loved him instead."

Carina flushed and Marcus, from his armchair, gave a short, unamused laugh. "That," he muttered, "will be the day."

Carina moved the footstool nearer to Ernest and farther away from Marcus. "You're the man in my life, Mr. de Verrier," she said, laughing.

"Am I, my dear? I'm not so sure. I've missed you, Carrie. The old people miss you, too. They keep asking me, where's your nice young lady gone? Has she got tired of us? I keep explaining you're learning to sing properly now and that my grandson's teaching you. And they say, 'Your grandson? Is she going to marry him and really be your granddaughter?' I say, not likely, she's meant for greater things in life than just marrying into the hard-up de Verrier family. Never had much money, the de Verriers, despite their grand name."

Carina stroked the braid that edged the worn fabric of Ernest's armchair. Her fingers fidgeted with it so restlessly that Ernest's hand came down and stopped her. "Miss your guitar, lass?" She nodded. "Sing to me, Carrie. Anything. I don't care what."

"I can't, Mr. de Verrier, I can't sing unaccompanied."

"You said that once before, Carina," came from the depths of the other armchair. "We've come a long way since then. Sing, Carina." With all her being she resisted the command in that voice. "Why else," it came again, "are you learning to sing if not to give pleasure to others?"

She knew he would win in the end. He usually did. "What shall I sing?" She even allowed him to make up her mind for her now.

"Roger Quilter's *Now sleeps the crimson petal*, Carina."

So she sang, uncertain at first, the haunting quality at last forcing its way through her nervousness in the second verse, giving the words an even greater poignancy.

Now folds the lily all her sweetness up.
And slips into the bosom of the lake
So fold thyself, my dearest, thou, and slip
Into my bosom and be lost in me.

There was a long, deep silence, that silence to which she

had grown so accustomed in the past but which she had almost forgotten. It was a tribute far greater than applause. And she knew, as Marcus must have known, to whom she had been singing.

CHAPTER SIX

MARCUS'S friendship with Faith Ringstead continued. They were often together. It was almost as if Marcus was using her as a barricade to keep some unknown danger at bay. When Carina passed them in the corridor, she averted her eyes, but not before she had seen Marcus's concentrated forward stare and the smile that creased his companion's pale face. She seemed to be laughing at some ironic joke against the Ascott girl which she hugged to herself because it gave her so much pleasure.

A tension had crept into the singing lessons which Carina had once enjoyed so much. It was impeding her progress. She knew she was not giving of her best and it was her old problem of an unsympathetic atmosphere. Paradoxical that the one who, above all, should be the prime element in dispelling such a feeling should be the source of it.

Marcus asked her one day, "Are your parents coming to the concert to hear you sing?"

"No. Since it's a lunchtime concert, my father will be at work, and my mother otherwise engaged."

"What is their attitude to your singing?"

"They take no interest."

"Having met your parents, and from what you have told me about their attitude to what you are doing, I'm deeply puzzled. Where has your voice come from? A natural voice such as yours doesn't occur out of the blue. It's usually passed down the generations in one way or another. Your mother has never sung, nor your father?" She shook her head. "Your grandparents, perhaps," the slight flinch she made surprised him, "or your great-grandparents?"

"I don't know!" she cried, unable to stand his questions, "I don't know where my voice came from."

He was astonished by her violent response but continued, "Have your mother and father any appreciation of music at all?"

"No. They both seem to be tone-deaf."

He sighed. "From all you say, I'm afraid I shall have to harden myself to the inevitable. And that is that you won't stay the course."

She was dismayed by his defeatist attitude, that he could have so little faith in her integrity after all this time and in spite of her efforts to rise to his high standards. "How can you talk like that when I've given up so much to please you?"

"I'm sorry." He said it mechanically, as though he was not convinced.

Carina's performance at the concert was well received. Ernest was there, of course, self-effacingly near the back as usual. She sang to him. Her hands were clasped tightly – too tightly – in front of her. Even now, and in spite of Marcus's sensitive accompaniment, she knew she was missing the reassurance of feeling her guitar in her hands. There was tension inside her, but she did her best to overcome it and, judging by the warmth and length of the applause at the end, she felt she must have succeeded.

It was not until next day, at her singing lesson, that she was given a true evaluation of her performance at the concert. Marcus ripped it to pieces.

"Your singing was mechanical. There was no feeling in it, no thought behind it. The songs came from your lips but not your mind. Your vowels were badly formed, your breathing was not properly controlled. Heaven knows," he stormed, "it's been an uphill effort so far, but my God, to think of having to go back to the foot of the hill, not even half-way up!"

She was white with disbelief; his words were eating into her, destroying her confidence like spilt acid. "You're only saying it to hurt me," she said.

"Look, Carina," his anger was under control now, "if I were to tell you that you'd put over a wonderful performance yesterday, I should not only be lying, I would be guilty of criminal negligence as your singing instructor. If I, as your teacher, don't criticise your work, who else is there to do it, to tell you the truth? I can't give praise where no praise is due."

She said sulkily, "It wasn't all that bad."

Her attitude of trying to find excuses aroused his anger again. "If you can say that, if you can persist in deluding yourself like this, then things are even worse than I thought. At least reasonable self-criticism would be one important step towards an improvement. It's quite obvious you didn't listen to yourself."

"The audience applauded me. They seemed to enjoy it."

"Of course they did, because they were an unsophisticated audience, consisting of mothers and fathers – and grandfathers. Ready to make allowances and to praise anyone in order to give encouragement."

"Which is something I don't get from you any more," she retorted. "If I didn't sing well, it was because of your lack of sympathy. I told you a long time ago I couldn't sing unless my listeners were sympathetic –"

"My dear girl," he confronted her, "your voice, your technique and your nerves should be good enough now to override your so-called and, if I may say so, childish need for the 'sympathetic atmosphere' you keep talking about. You must harden yourself to 'atmospheres'. Grow up, Carina, have more self-confidence, more self-reliance. Ironic, isn't it, that I should have to tell *you* this, with your upbringing and your secure background? You've got no fight, Carina, no guts. The security behind you has made any sort of struggle, whether against mental or physical odds so unnecessary, you don't know how to surmount an obstacle when you meet it."

She was choking with tears, reeling under the impact of his words and his unkindness. He, Marcus de Verrier, the man in whose hands she had placed herself as trustingly as a babe in arms trusts its mother's hold, was writing her off as a failure. He was flinging accusations at her, making false charges against her character.

She had given up fighting the tears, they were pouring down her cheeks. "So you're as good as telling me that because of my so-called 'cushioned' upbringing I'll never make a singer, no matter how hard I try. How little you know about me," she cried, "how little you know!" She went to the door.

"Where are you going?"

"Home. I can't sing for you any more. I shall never sing again."

"I've heard that before from so many others. You'll get over it, you'll come round."

"Never," she sobbed, "never."

Carina was alone at dinner that evening, which pleased her as she did not have to make pleasant, polite conversation. Afterwards she put her guitar in the back seat of the car and drove to Ernest de Verrier's. She saw with relief that Marcus's car was missing from the driveway, which meant he was out.

As she entered the living-room, Ernest could see the state she was in. She sat on the footstool and it all came tumbling out – the things Marcus had said, her uncertainties, her sense of failure, her decision to give it all up. Patiently Ernest tried to pick up the pieces of her shattered confidence, but even after he had retrieved them, he knew it was no good. They could not be put together again to make a whole. This was going to be a repair job which would take all his skill.

110

"Come on, Mr. de Verrier," Carina said, "we're going to your club. And," defiance lifted her head, "I'm going to sing to them, if they'll have me."

"Carrie dear," Ernest put out a hand, trembling a little, "don't go. You know what Marcus will say."

"I don't *care* what Marcus says, Mr. de Verrier. I don't *care* any more." She linked her arm in his and started to pull him from the chair. "Come with me. If you don't, I shall still go."

He let her help him up. Suddenly he looked frail and old. There was a stab of fear inside her that almost made her double up with pain. Had she done this to him? Should she force him to go against his will?

He felt her hesitate and said, "Come along, lass, we'll both go. I won't let you down."

Carina received a boisterous welcome. She took her guitar on to the platform and sang, defiantly, in the old way, the old songs, singing with a passion that moved them to tears.

Ernest was dabbing at his eyes when she went to stand beside him. "You're a bad lass, Carrie," he mumbled, "but you're a great lass, too. I don't know what my grandson will say to you."

"He won't know, Mr. de Verrier, will he?"

"Rest assured, Carrie, I won't tell him."

She drove him home and sat on the footstool at his feet, holding her guitar as though it was a beloved pet that had strayed and come home again. She plucked at it, thinking back to her performance. Now that the euphoria of defiance was passing, guilt began to edge its way in, toning down all the colours in her mind, freezing out the warmth which had been engendered by the audience's rapturous reception. She had broken all the rules, she had turned her back on all the training Marcus had so painstakingly given her. It was as though she had clicked contemptuous fingers in front of his eyes.

She thought she heard a noise outside. Was it Marcus's

car? Fear struck her like forked lightning running through her body. She stood up, looking for somewhere to hide, but she heard a front door open and close across the street. She relaxed.

"Did you think it was Marcus?" Ernest laughed. "He won't be back yet. He's out with his Faith woman. Hope and Charity isn't in it. Can't stand her. She's got a figure like she's wrapped all the time in an eiderdown and eyes as cunning as a fox."

"A fox is male, Mr. de Verrier," Carina corrected, sitting down again. "You mean a vixen."

"Vixen's right, lass. He must be out of his mind to trail her around with him. They've gone to a concert. Expect they'll eat somewhere afterwards. That's what young people do nowadays, isn't it?"

Carina's shoulders lifted hopelessly. "Perhaps." She put her guitar aside. "I'll make some tea."

As they drank it, Ernest said, "We all suffer from self-doubt, Carrie, especially when we're young. And we all learn from our failures. You know tailoring was my trade? I was an apprentice lad, way back in the old days, when so much was done by hand – not like your dad's clothes. High-class his stuff may be, but there's a lot of work on them done by machine that once took us hours to do by hand, in poor light and even poorer conditions. Well," he took a sip of tea, "my first suit was a complete failure. It was torn to bits by my boss, and I was as good as torn to bits by his tongue." He glanced at her and saw the depression lifting from her face, so he talked on. "I nearly threw the job in, but someone who'd been in the game years told me not to be a fool. He encouraged me and got my fighting spirit going again. I'll never forget that man, although I've forgotten his name. I can still remember his face, though, as plain as if it were in front of me now."

She put the cool back of the guitar against her burning cheek. "It was the way Marcus said it, Mr. de Verrier. He said some terrible things."

"Oh, I don't suppose they were all that bad, Carrie. He may have been a bit rough with you, but — well, he seems to be under a strain at the moment. Don't know why. Work's getting him down, probably." He shifted sideways. "Tell you what, you go and see him in the morning, when you've both cooled down, and talk it over with him. I won't tell him what you did tonight, so you can pretend it never happened. All right, lass?"

The key turned in the front door. Carina was paralysed with fright and even Ernest looked worried. Marcus was in the room before she had a chance to move. He must have seen her car outside. The telltale guitar was in her lap, the revealing colour was in her cheeks and the give-away fear sat squarely in her eyes.

Marcus looked at her, then at his grandfather, and finally at the guitar. The waves of dread emanating from the occupants of the room reached out to him and sucked him in. He was in the water before he knew where he was and the currents were drawing him under.

They both waited for him to speak first. Carina crouched forward as if trying to hide the guitar with her body.

"Don't tell me," he said, moving slowly towards her, "you have reverted. You've returned to your old ways. I know what you've been doing — you've been out singing. With that." He looked as his grandfather. "Am I right?"

Ernest sat, stiff and straight, keeping his vow of silence.

Marcus turned to Carina, towering over her. "After all the promises you made never to go back to it, after all I have told you about the dangers of singing in the wrong way. Shall I tell you something else? No voice, however strong, can be maltreated with impunity. In fact, the more beautiful the voice, the more likely it is to suffer from ill-treatment. The velvet quality which some voices have, and which you are lucky enough to possess, can be quite destroyed by persistent disregard of the rules. Now do you see what you're risking?"

Carina said in a colourless tone, "It doesn't matter any

more. I told you, I'm giving up singing."

"But, lass," Ernest said, unable to stay quiet, and feeling that all his efforts to restore her confidence were being trampled into the ground, "you can't do this to yourself." He knew by her quick shrug that such an appeal would have no effect, so he changed it. "You can't do this to *me*, Carrie."

He saw her waver, sensed her vacillation. He sat forward, hopeful, waiting. He made one more effort. "Can you, Carrie?"

She frowned, looked at him, began to capitulate, said, "Well, I –"

"I said you had no guts, *and I was right!*" The words came coldly, disastrously from his grandson. "You crumple at the slightest opposition, the merest hint of difficulty."

The memory of the struggle she had had with herself to accept his point of view, of the many concessions and sacrifices she had made in order to please him and fall in with his wishes, flashed through her mind like a fast-moving film. It proved to be the breaking point.

"How you can stand there," she shrieked, "and call me cowardly, after all I've – all I've . . ."

Her control gave way like a barrier under a stampeding crowd, grinding into the dust all reason and common sense. She stood, lifted her guitar and crashed it to the floor. It lay there, destroyed and lifeless, like a wild animal brought down by a bullet. She looked at it, aghast at what she had done, then raised blazing eyes to the man who had made her do it.

Fury set her mind spinning like a top. She hurled herself upon him, intending to hurt him as catastrophically as he had hurt her. But he parried the blow of her body against his and caught her wrists and held them. Even as she struggled to free herself, she was forced to recognise his greater strength. She had to acknowledge that physically as well as mentally, he was her superior.

She went slack and he let her go. She began to sob.

"Carrie?" She ran to Ernest, knelt down and put her head on his lap. As she sobbed, he stroked her hair, comforting her and saying, "There, there, lass, don't take it to heart like that." He looked up at his grandson who was standing by the door.

"Go easy on her, lad, go easy. Don't destroy her, Marcus. I told you before, she needs support. I've never known a girl need bolstering up as much as she does."

Marcus bent slowly as though, in the space of a few minutes, years had been added to his age. He picked up the broken guitar and looked it over as if trying to find a way of mending it. But he seemed to admit in the end that it was beyond repair. He placed it on the footstool and went away.

Carina did not see Marcus again until her next singing lesson a few days later. She apologised for what had taken place between them at his grandfather's house.

"The sorrow is mutual," he replied stiffly. "Please accept *my* apologies for my temporary loss of tact and courtesy." He forced a smile. "It only goes to prove that I, too, am human. And also that I'm not immune any more than you are to that accursed thing called artistic temperament." He brushed back his hair with both hands, the gesture of someone with too much on his mind. "This is your last singing lesson before the end of term." He thrust his hands in his pockets and stared at the floor as if it held an enormous fascination for him. "Next term Miss Ringstead will take over your piano lessons again." Carina made a faint movement of protest but said nothing. "And in the New Year another teacher will probably be taking over your singing. I shall think about it over Christmas."

This time she translated her protest into words. "But why, Marcus, why?"

"Things have reached an impasse between us, Carina. Our temperaments seem to be irreconcilable. As I told you at the start, teacher and student must work as a team. There must be complete trust, friendliness and sympathy

115

between them. One can hardly say that our relationship contains any of those qualities. We can't go on like this." He raised his head and saw the tears threatening. "I'm sorry, but it's no use, Carina." His voice was firm. "When I see you next term, I shall tell you of my decision. Go home, now."

There was no arguing with him. He was in charge, he was the teacher. She, as the student, had to do his bidding. She left him staring out of the window, his broad back bent as if he had the weight of the world upon it.

Carina knew as soon as she went in to the house that Justine was home. She knew by the perfume hanging on the air. But she did not seek her sister out. Instead she raced upstairs to her room, shut herself in and cried her heart out. Which was where Justine found her some time later.

"It can only be," said Justine, slim, blonde and attractive, "a man. No woman cries like that for any other reason."

Carina turned her head on the pillow and opened her tear-puffed eyes. She had not seen Justine for some time. She sat up, pushing her damp hair from her blotched cheeks. "Sorry, Justine. Nice to see you."

"Don't tell lies, and tell little sister all about it instead." Justine sat beside her, sandwiching a box of eye-shadow between her palms. "Is it a man?"

"If you must know, yes." Trying to change the subject, Carina asked, "How are things with you?"

"Couldn't be better, unlike things with you. Is it Avery?"

"No."

Justine went to the mirror and started applying the eye-shadow as thickly as a glazier pressing putty around a window-pane. "Then who? Don't keep me in suspense, darling. At least tell me his name. He really must be something if he causes you all that bother."

"Marcus." Having gone so far, Carina decided to apply

116

the rest. "de Verrier. He's teaching me singing."

"Oh, God," said Justine to her bored reflection, "not the same old teacher-student syndrome? Haven't you got past the infatuation stage in your emotional development yet? You're a big girl now, five years older than I am. What are the parents' reactions?"

"Nil. There's nothing to react to."

"So it's unrequited love and all that rubbish." She swung round, her blonde hair swirling out. "Want little sister to give you a few tips on how to make him requite it?"

"No good. Too many obstacles in the way. Trying to reach him is like a mountain climber trying to stretch across and reach someone on another mountain top."

"Give it up. Find yourself a man, not a puny, half-baked teacher."

"If you'd seen him, you wouldn't speak of him like that."

"Is he something? Got a picture? Nothing?"

"Nothing. He's head of the music school."

"How old?"

"Thirty-one." She gave Justine a sisterly smile. "Unmarried, unattached and untouchable. Tall, dark *and* handsome."

"Lead me to him, sister!"

"You wouldn't stand a chance. He's got this thing about money. Can't stand the thought of all that wealth in the Ascott family's bank account."

"But it isn't your money, any more than it's my money."

"It's not so much the money he dislikes as everything that goes with it."

"What's wrong with what goes with it? It's just great having an allowance some families have to live on." Carina felt a little sick. "Tell me, has he met the parents?"

"Yes. He wasn't impressed."

Justine laughed. "Can't say I'm surprised." She turned

117

back to study her reflection. "You know, you're lucky, Carina. You're not their 'blood daughter', as you put it. *You* haven't inherited some of their worst characteristics. You were the 'chosen' one, as they've always insisted on calling you. So desperately tactful and Freudian." She helped herself to Carina's powder.

Carina looked at her incredulously. Surely Justine wasn't jealous? If so, it must surely be the biggest irony of all time. "But," she placated, "that was only to make me feel 'wanted' after you came along."

Justine shrugged, leaving Carina in some doubt as to whether she had convinced her or not.

When Justine had gone, Carina dragged herself from the bed and searched in a drawer. She drew out a photograph, bent and finger-marked with much handling. On the back was written in a careful, flowing hand, "Us with our darling Carina, on her first birthday." She was perched on her father's – her real father's – shoulder, and her mother was gazing up at her and holding her hand. They were the only two people in the world to whom she had really belonged, her own parents who had loved her as Phyllis and Lloyd loved Justine. The picture, pressed to her cheek, became warm with her warmth, as if she were trying to infuse it with life.

She had found the photograph some years ago in the waste paper basket in Phyllis and Lloyd's bedroom. Instinct had made her pick it up. The horror and indignation she had felt at their callous action in throwing away something so precious had been a kind of turning point and she had never felt the same towards her adoptive parents again.

Now, years later, in her maturity, she thought she could see why they had done it. If they had given it to her, they had probably argued, it might have unsettled her and brought about a resurgence of painful and distressing memories. But they had been wrong. Just looking at those two happy people, gazing up at their baby – herself – gave her a greater sense of belonging, of possessing roots, than anything she had known since the terrible day those two people had been taken from her.

At dinner that evening, in the candlelight which flickered over the gleaming silver, crystal and white linen, Phyllis said hopefully to Carina, "Looking forward to seeing Avery again, darling?" Carina moved her shoulders, an action which could have indicated either indifference or acquiescence, according to the wishes of the onlooker. "You know we're having a party to announce your –"

"There's nothing to announce, Mother."

"Oh, but there will be, won't there? After all, you still wear Avery's ring."

"Only because it's safer on my finger than in a drawer in my room."

"Had a letter from Avery the other day," Lloyd said, tipping back his head and draining his wine glass. "It was about business, of course, but he added a postscript. 'Can't wait to get home again and see your beautiful daughter.' "

"Which one?" Justine drawled. "Didn't specify, I suppose. Left his options open in case he gets refused by one and can use the other as a fall-back."

Carina choked over her drink and had consequently to suffer the thuds on the back her sister thought fit to administer.

"The trouble is," Phyllis said, in a worried tone, "that the old saying about absence making the heart grow fonder is a lot of nonsense." To her husband, "Isn't there someone else you could send out to South America in place of Avery? Then he could stay at home and we could have an Easter wedding."

The two sisters exchanged hopeless glances.

"No," her husband answered snappily, annoyed as he usually was when his wife – or anyone else – tried to interfere with the running of the business, "there's no one else. If he wants promotion to a directorship when he –" he glanced obliquely at his recalcitrant daughter, "when he takes his place as a member of the family, then he's got to learn the hard way. If he possesses any pioneering spirit, and he'd damned well better, then it will show itself out there. He won't be welcome as a son-in-law if he hasn't got guts."

"Of course, darling," his wife soothed, "of course he's got – er – guts."

"He'll need them," murmured Justine into her table napkin, "if only to help him cope with an unwilling wife."

"Unwilling?" Phyllis was shocked. "Of course Carina won't be unwilling. One look at Avery and she'll fall into his arms!"

But on the day of Avery's return, Carina did not fall into his arms. She locked herself in her room. She heard him wandering about downstairs like an animal restless for its mate. Her father's voice seemed to be telling him to stop. A few words were exchanged and footsteps trod the stairs, then came a tap on her door.

"Let me in, Carina," Avery's voice pleaded. "I – I want to talk to you."

"But I don't want to talk to *you*," Carina called.

"At least let's discuss things," Avery urged. "I've – I've had second thoughts."

The door was flung wide and a bright smile greeted him. "So have I," said Carina. "Had second thoughts."

"Oh," said Avery, coming in. He saw the ring on the dressing-table and grinned. "Why have you put that in such a strategic position? So that I can slip it on the correct finger this time?"

"You said," she accused, "you'd had second thoughts."

"I know. But I had to get in the room somehow, didn't I?"

She frowned, comparing in her mind the selfish blue eyes, the petulant lips and the delicately structured, slightly effeminate face with the sensitivity and strength of Marcus's. "So you lied?"

He shrugged, tossing back his long, pale brown hair. "Your father suggested it as a means of gaining entry."

"He would. He knows how I feel about you."

"Which is?"

"Nothing doing." She nodded to the ring. "It's yours."

"Wrong. It's yours." He held her left hand and tried to force the ring on her engagement finger, but she tore her hand away.

"I said, nothing doing."

"You're going to marry me, so stop fooling, Carina."

Her brown eyes were both challenging and amusing. "How are you going to make me?"

He stared at her, nonplussed, and she laughed at his expression. She knew she was the link between himself and the directorship her father had promised him on his marriage to her, and felt just a tinge of pity because he was now in the process of seeing the position he coveted slip out of his reach. But she was not going to be "used" by him to gain his ends. Not only did she not love the man, she did not even like him.

"There's one way," he said between his teeth, "to help me get what I want." Before she knew what he was about, he had pushed her down on to the bed, but it took him all his strength to keep her there because she resisted with all hers.

"Stop acting out of character, Avery," she said, short of breath but surprisingly calm in view of what was happening to her. "If you think you can achieve your objective this way . . ."

"It *is* my character, darling," he responded smoothly. "I always get what I want in the end. You'll learn that after we're married."

"That *does* endear me to you!"

"So you're laughing at me, are you?" His lips pressed down, but she failed to respond. "You can say 'no' as much as you like, Carina, but I'm going to get you, and marry you. You've got the blood of the Ascotts in your veins and that's good enough for me – and the kids we shall have."

As he struggled with her, his lips moved feverishly and

121

he whispered to himself, "I'd do anything to get accepted into the Ascott family."

"Even rape?" came the muffled voice beneath him.

He raised his head in astonishment, and blushed boyishly. "Sorry. I didn't look at it that way." He lifted himself away from her and she dusted herself down, swinging her legs round and sitting beside him on the bed.

"Why not try your luck with Justine?"

"You're the one I want. And love," he added as an afterthought. "You're the deep one. She's so shallow, so obvious."

"You'd be better off with her, Avery. After all, she really is one of the family. I'm not." She caught her breath. She had given away her most guarded secret.

"What do you mean, you're not, but she is?"

Carina had no option now but to explain. "I'm adopted."

She waited for his declaration of undying love for her, saying he wanted to marry her more than ever, his beautiful orphan, his little stray.

"You're *what*?" He bounded off the bed as if he were sitting on a drawing pin. "You're not telling me you're illegitimate?"

She laughed uproariously. She had held the trump card all the time, without even knowing it. How easy it would have been to get rid of him from the start, if only she had used it earlier! "No, sorry to disappoint you. My parents were killed in a road accident years ago. I survived. The Ascotts adopted me." The bare facts, nothing of the underlying miseries, some of which were so imprinted on her childhood memory she could still recall the horror.

"My father was an employee of Lloyd Ascott. He was an under-manager at one of the Ascott factories. So you see, he was an employee of theirs, a worker," she added, rubbing it in, "a member of the *working* class. The Ascotts knew my parents had left a small daughter – me – and they wanted a child badly, so they adopted me."

"No wonder," said the gallant Avery, "they wanted to

marry you off."

"Thanks," she said mildly, handing him the ring which he accepted without demur. "Now perhaps you'll take my advice and try your luck with Justine. It's as well you've got a second string to your bow, isn't it, to help you achieve the goal you want so much?"

She swept out of the room with Avery trailing behind. Her mother looked up from the hall and saw the glow of contentment on Carina's face. "It's all settled, darling?" she asked.

"Yes, Mother," said Carina expansively, "it's all settled. It's all off."

"No! But, Carina, the engagement party . . ."

Justine emerged from the dining-room. "Avery, there she is," Carina grinned at him, "catch her while she's in a good mood." To her mother, "You never know, you might still have your engagement party!"

Justine, looking from one to the other, recognised the clues, sifted swiftly through the evidence, made a speedy deduction and turned and ran. Avery sped after her.

There was a party, but no engagement. Avery had stayed on over the Christmas holiday, despite the fact that, for the moment anyway, he was no longer a prospective son-in-law.

The party was in full swing when the telephone rang. Carina, who had opted out and was sitting alone in an armchair in the lounge hall, answered it.

"Carrie?" Her heart leapt, her pulses raced. A voice from the de Verrier family! "We've missed you over Christmas, lass. Are you free for a bit, Carrie? Could you call and see us? My son and his wife are here. They want to meet my lady-friend!"

She laughed. She was so happy she could cry. "Marcus's parents? Yes, Mr. de Verrier," she lowered her voice as she did not want to be overheard, "I'm free. I'll come straight away."

"Good. What's that noise, Carrie? You haven't got company?"

"Oh," she said airily, "someone's put a record on. See you in a few minutes."

She found her handbag with the car keys in it, pulled on the first coat she could lay her hands on – it happened to be the fur coat her parents had given her for her eighteenth birthday – and ran out to her car. She was away down the road in the darkness before her parents could stop her.

It was New Year's Eve and houses were gay with coloured lights and decorated trees. She parked her car outside Ernest's house and it was not until she was getting out and her coat fell open that she realised she was still wearing the long, clinging white dress she had put on for the party. It would, she knew, build an immediate barrier between herself and Marcus's parents. It looked what it was – a costly and beautiful example of an Ascott model gown.

The door was on the catch as usual, but on this occasion she was too shy to push and enter as she usually did. Someone was coming to answer the bell. Was it Marcus?

It was a woman bearing a remarkable resemblance to him. She was smiling warmly. If she noticed the luxurious fur coat adorning the girl on the doorstep she gave no sign. "Welcome, Miss Ascott," she said, pulling the door wide, "nice of you to spare the time. I'm Marcus's mother, Edith."

"And I'm Carina. Please call me that." Carina took off her coat and hung it in the hall cupboard, then turned apprehensively to witness the upraised de Verrier eyebrows and the de Verrier contempt for costly things. But the eyes that looked at her now held praise, and the smile was full of pleasure. No censure there.

"What a simply beautiful dress, my dear! You look wonderful in it. One of your father's?"

Carina nodded, relaxing happily under the woman's warmth and sincerity. No need to apologise to this unaffected, spontaneous person.

Edith de Verrier was tall for a woman – she had to be to have a son of Marcus's height. She was slim for her age, too, and vigorous in mind and manner.

Carina felt her habitual reserve crumbling away. "To be honest, Mrs. de Verrier, I was delighted to get away from home. There was a party, and I hate parties."

They were in the living-room now. There was Ernest in his usual armchair, his face bright as he looked at the girl who came in. He held out a hand and Carina took it, bending down to kiss his cheek. She straightened and looked round. No Marcus, but a man almost as tall, his hair receding, his face round and full, his body well-built, with a touch of Ernest in his expression. In his eyes was the good humour of Marcus, when Marcus chose to be good-humoured, which was not very often.

His hand came out and his grip was firm. "Carrie? Carina? Which is it?" Carina told him. "Two personalities in one. My father tells me you're a grand little lass who needs careful handling, my son tells me you're an obstinate little so-and-so with a beautiful voice. Now who am I to believe?"

They all laughed, even Marcus, who had appeared at the door. Carina swung round, eager for the sight of him. He was scrutinising her from top to toe, he of all the family was building that wall, was making her embarrassed about the way she was dressed, and – almost – ashamed. Only Marcus could do that to her, no one else.

"Party, did you say?" asked Marcus.

"Yes." She looked down at herself. "That's why I'm dressed like this. I'm sorry, but I didn't have time to change."

"Sorry?" exclaimed Marcus's father. "For goodness' sake don't apologise! It's our pleasure."

"Whose party?" asked Marcus, his eyes still touched with cynicism. "Yours? To announce your engagement?"

"That was its original intention, but there was no engagement to announce. I turned Avery down."

125

"Lovers' quarrel?" asked John de Verrier.

"No. We had a – a difference of opinion, so different it was irreconcilable."

"You'll make it up," said Edith, with confidence. "Lovers always do."

Marcus was staring. He lifted Carina's right hand and raised his eyebrows. "Gone?"

"Yes. I told you, no engagement, nothing."

The action and exchange were touched with an intimacy which did not escape the watchful eyes of Marcus's parents. Ernest was not even looking. It was as if he knew all there was to know.

"Sit down, Carrie," Ernest urged, "make yourself at home. You usually do."

Carina took her place on the footstool, shaking her head at the chair which John de Verrier had gallantly offered her.

"Are you," John asked, "the young lady whose guitar stands in a corner in Marcus's room, looking very sorry for itself?"

"Is that where it is?" Carina murmured. "Yes. I – dropped it."

"I've been looking at it," John went on, "to see if it could be repaired. You know I sell musical instruments? Sometimes we can work miracles." Carina looked at him hopefully. "But no good, I'm afraid. It must have had a nasty knock."

Marcus cracked the awkward silence with the crunch of a brazil nut shell between the jaws of the nutcrackers. He extracted the nut whole, looked pleased with himself and moved to stand behind Carina. She tilted her head back to look up at him. He popped the nut between her parted lips and went away.

"Thanks," she mumbled, her mouth full, conscious of those watching eyes.

"Have a good Christmas, Carina?" Marcus asked, from a distance. "Lots of lovely presents?"

She heard the derisive note and answered flatly, "Lots and lots."

Edith, sensing an atmosphere without understanding why, took up the subject with enthusiasm and they talked Christmas for some time. Then they talked music and more music. Carina joined in, her eyes bright, her cheeks flushed with excitement – wasn't Marcus there, and his parents, not to mention his grandfather? And wasn't she amongst them, in the heart of the family, as though she belonged?

"Won't your family miss you, Carina?" Edith asked, jolting her back to reality as painfully as a baby falling from its mother's arms.

"Possibly. They don't even know where I am. But they won't worry. They're used to my unpredictable ways. Like a bad penny, I always turn up again."

"Bad *penny*, Carina?" The mocking note was there again. "Aren't you undervaluing yourself a little? I know for certain you're worth a small fortune."

She turned to make a biting reply, but Marcus had left the room. The others began talking of family matters and Carina, murmuring her excuses, went to find him. He was in the kitchen sharpening a pencil into the pedal bin.

"Marcus?" She stood beside him. "Have you – thought, yet?"

"What about? Your singing lessons?"

"Yes." She held her breath and gazed up into his face.

He flicked her a glance, taking in the provocation of her shape, her dark, glowing beauty, her anxiety, the way her eyes – those maddening eyes – were willing him to give an answer, the right answer. And he kept her waiting.

"The party mood suits you," he murmured, "it gives you an animation which makes you doubly attractive. Irresistible, in fact. If it weren't for all that stood between us . . ."

"Marcus!" she pleaded, "stop teasing. Please tell me."

He pared away at the wood of the pencil as if his life depended on it. "I've thought about the subject a great deal," he said at last.

"And – what have you decided?"

Now he scraped at the point and fine black dust showered into the bin. "Tell me, what would you do if I handed you over to someone else?"

"I'd give up."

"Just like that?"

"Just like that. I'd – lose interest."

"As you did in commerce and art?" There he was, bringing up her past mistakes again. "So I'm the motivating force where your singing is concerned?"

She frowned, considering the question. "Yes, I suppose you must be."

"That," he said softly, "is quite an admission, if you but knew it." He lifted his foot from the pedal and the lid of the bin snapped shut. "Well, Carina," he slid the pencil into his top pocket, "what are we to do about this explosive situation between us? This love-hate relationship?" The blade of the penknife folded with a satisfying click into its metal casing and he pushed it into his trouser pocket.

"I didn't know," she said slowly, "there was any 'hate' about it." He smiled at the second giveaway statement of the evening. She looked at him. "I can't think why you hate me?" He smiled again. "Can't we just be friends?"

"Even friends quarrel sometimes, Carina."

She smiled at him brightly, optimistically. "Then that would be just right, wouldn't it?"

He laughed loudly and his mother appeared. "Hallo, you two. What are you up to?"

"Unfortunately," said her son cryptically, his eyes lingering on the attractions of the girl beside him, "nothing."

"Come along, Carina," Mrs. de Verrier linked arms with her, "come back to the bosom of the family."

And Carina did.

It was when she was leaving at half an hour to midnight that Ernest said, pointing to the mistletoe hanging from the hall ceiling,

"Quick, Marcus, catch her before she goes."

"That's right," said Edith, "then I'll know I didn't spend my money on it for nothing."

Marcus looked up at the mistletoe and down at the doubtful face he was being encouraged to kiss.

"If you don't," said his father, "I will. With my wife's permission, of course!"

"Go on, Marcus," his grandfather urged. "A kiss for luck. It *is* New Year's Eve."

"So it is," said his grandson. His hand clamped on Carina's wrist, preventing the escape she seemed to be contemplating, and he pulled her into the hall, closing the living-room door behind him. He smiled wickedly. "You never know, if you submit to my demands you might even succeed in persuading me not to hand your singing lessons over to someone else. It's not exactly unknown for a woman to use her feminine attractions to get something she wanted from a man." He took her into his arms and whispered, his lips against hers, "Happy New Year, Carina." She made one more effort to get away, but his arms merely tightened. "Come along now," he said, "kiss teacher."

The kiss, potent, compelling, swamped her senses, his hold upon her too powerful to permit even the beginnings of a struggle.

"Marcus," she gasped at last, attempting to free herself, "how could you!"

"How could I what?" His eyes, laughing at her, moved over her features, coming to rest on her eyes. It was almost as if he were staring in at two windows, and was trying to guess what was going on inside the room. "How could I take advantage of the situation — and of you? Did you really expect me to let such an opportunity go? With all the ingredients for a feast, the time, the place, the family cheering on the sidelines, the girl, beautiful, vibrant, willing . . ."

"I was *not* willing!"

"Weren't you, my sweet one? But you were. I'll show

you just how willing —" His head came down again, but this time she did not stay passive. She dragged her lips from his, used every muscle in her body to achieve her end and got away from him, running out into the darkness.

CHAPTER SEVEN

THE New Year had been celebrated and was behind them. Justine returned to her finishing school, Carina to her studies. During the first week of term, Marcus was noticeable by his absence. She knew he was there because she often heard his voice, either echoing along the corridors or behind the door of his office.

Carina longed to see him because she wanted to be put out of her misery. What had he decided to do about her singing lessons?

Faith Ringstead became her piano teacher again. It was sheer misery to have the dull, unresponsive woman sitting beside her, trying to convert her back to her old mechanical way of playing. Faith did comment, grudgingly, that there had been some improvement in technique and touch – Carina supposed she paid the compliment only because it would have reflected badly on Marcus if she had not. But she needed to work much harder, Faith said, if she wanted to pass the examination.

At the end of the week, as Carina approached the music room for her singing lesson, she found to her dismay that she was shaking. She opened the door. The room was empty and she experienced temporary relief that there was no strange teacher awaiting her. But as the time passed and Marcus did not come, the apprehension returned.

Footsteps came striding along the corridor and the door

came open. Carina's heart lifted like a lark rising. Marcus smiled broadly – her pleasure was manifest – and took his seat at the piano. She could not speak for relief.

He extended his hand towards her. "Friends, Carina?"

"Friends, Marcus." Their hands met, held and parted.

Marcus was coaching her for another college concert, the second of the academic year. She had better be good this time, he told her, or else . . . Or else he would probably put her across his knee.

Their relations remained surprisingly cordial. His teaching was inspiring, her response, he said, was magnificent. Now her voice was improving beyond all expectations. It was coming into its own at last. It possessed a fullness and a purity which even he had not dreamed was there, and again he asked her, in a puzzled way, where in heaven's name her voice had come from. Which side of the family? Could Justine sing, or any of her grandparents?

When he asked such questions she closed up as resolutely as a shopkeeper shutting up for the night. She bolted and barred the door to him – and pulled down the blinds. It was, however, the only time she retreated into herself, keeping him out. At all other times there was an accord between them which formed them into a perfect team.

Marcus told Carina one day that he was taking a group of students to a concert in London. "I should like you to come with us. An old friend of mine," he named a well-known woman singer, "is performing. I knew her in the old days when I was active in the world of music. Besides being a concert pianist, I was sometimes invited to conduct, and she sang under my conductorship. I should like you to hear her and if possible to meet her. You'll come?"

"Yes, please," Carina answered, and he laughed at her eagerness.

They collected in a group at the railway station. It was a Saturday afternoon in March and the weather was blustery. Marcus arrived and made for Carina, but the others swarmed round him and he was cut off from her. She wished he were not so popular. She wished she were more pushing and did not have this maddening tendency to hold back, letting others overtake.

Even on the train journey Marcus was separated from her. Her companion for most of the way was a young man whose main subject was the violin. He was not very communicative, but when they did converse it was about music. Near the end of the journey Marcus strolled along and stopped beside her companion who was seated next to the gangway. They talked for a few minutes while Carina stared out of the window.

"Are you with us, Carina?" At the sound of Marcus's voice, half mocking, half reprimand, her heart did a crash stop. Then it thudded on in top gear.

"Sorry," she managed a smile, "I was just thinking."

"It's good to know you do think now and then!" It was meant as a joke, and the others laughed, but Carina took it the wrong way. She gave him a reproachful look and turned back to the window.

At the concert hall, in the foyer, Marcus showed Carina his ticket, comparing its number with hers. "We're together," he said, smiling like a man who had just played a bountiful Santa Claus and had given her exactly the present she wanted.

She forced her eyebrows up into two supercilious arches and swept ahead. She could afford to appear indifferent now she knew they would be sitting together.

The hall was full, the audience appreciative of each item. Marcus's friend — her name was Fleur Leeson — was to appear in the second half.

In the interval, Marcus thrust a large and costly box of chocolates into Carina's arms. "For me, Marcus?"

"For you." He whispered in her ear, "With my love."

"Don't be silly," she said, frowning.

Still in an undertone he asked, his eyes mocking, "You think I'm not capable of loving?"

"How do I know?" she answered fiercely. "It's a subject

133

that will never concern me. If you'd asked me if you were capable of hating I'd have said 'yes' three times over."

"Oh?" The de Verrier eyebrows lifted. "And who exactly do I hate?"

"Me. Who else?"

His hand reached out for the box on her lap. "If that's all the thanks I get –"

"No, no!" She pushed his hand away. "Don't take them back. I'm sorry for seeming ungrateful. Thank you for giving them to me." She opened the lid and thrust the box towards him. "Have one."

He smiled. "With your love?"

She coloured, hoping the subdued lighting in the auditorium would hide her embarrassment. "With my love."

"Now it will taste all the sweeter," he mocked. But instead of taking a chocolate he passed the box along the row to the others, having first asked Carina's permission. When the chocolates were returned, he enquired, "Which one do you fancy, Carina?"

"Well," she looked over his shoulder, "if it's still there I like the coffee best, but if you want it –"

He selected it, held it in front of her lips until they parted, then he pushed the sweet between them. The others laughed.

"You're always feeding me," she mumbled, her mouth full of melting chocolate.

"I only do it to keep you quiet," he said, amidst more laughter.

She could not reproach him, not with his giant box of chocolates in her arms.

Fleur Leeson swept on to the platform. She had beauty, presence and poise, and Carina, listening intently to the performance, escaped from herself and became one with the singer. So absorbed was she in every nuance of that beautiful voice that the applause at the end came as a shock and seemed a sacrilege. She turned shining eyes to the man beside her and he smiled back as if he had known all the time how she would react.

Backstage, Fleur Leeson was charm itself. She listened attentively to Marcus's assessment of Carina's voice and accepted with genuine pleasure his invitation to the school of music's next concert.

"I want you to hear her," Marcus said. "I should like to know what you think of her singing."

Fleur put her hand on his arm. "I remember the old days, Marcus, and how you encouraged me. You told me I would get to the top."

"And I was right."

She smiled charmingly. "That I cannot deny. And you think your Carina will get to the top?"

Marcus rested his hand on Carina's shoulder. "If she wants to get there, and wants it enough, yes."

"Then, Miss Ascott, to the top you will go," Fleur laughed. "My dear friend Marcus has wonderful judgement. Trust it, my dear. I did, and now," the sweep of her arm indicated the whole world, "you see where I am."

In the train on the way home, Marcus sat opposite Carina. He talked and joked with the others, but now and then his eyes rested on her as if wondering at her silence. One by one the other students left the train and then they were alone. Marcus moved to sit beside her.

"Still up in the clouds, Carina?"

She smiled. "Yes. I'm still on that platform, trying to imagine myself singing to that vast and critical London audience." She sighed. "I can't ever see myself doing it. I don't even know that I want to."

He answered sharply, "Of course you'll do it, and of course you will want to." His hand covered hers and his voice softened. "Why so shrinking suddenly?"

She shook her head because it was so difficult to put her feelings into words. "Those people would be beyond my reach. They wouldn't help me by giving me their warmth and understanding as the old people used to do."

135

"How can you say that? Didn't you hear the applause this afternoon? It was deafening."

"But Fleur Leeson is wonderful, and well-known. I'm neither."

"Give a London audience some credit, girl. I know by experience how much they encourage newcomers."

They sat in silence for some time, hands loosely linked, shoulders touching, swaying with the movement of the carriage. As the train drew into the station and stopped, Marcus helped her down on to the platform. She shivered in the cool evening air. His arm lifted and rested across her shoulders. "Can I take you somewhere for a meal, Carina?"

"It's kind of you, but no, thanks." She smiled brightly. "Let's go home," she said, and corrected herself quickly. "Your home, not mine."

"I never thought you meant otherwise," he commented dryly.

Arm round her or not, she thought, he could never forget her background. It was always just beneath the surface of his mind, erupting volcano-like, when least expected.

"I'll get us a meal," she offered.

"You will? You *can*?" There it was again, the studied disbelief.

"An omelette?" she asked Ernest, standing in front of him, glowing and excited, like a small girl.

"My mouth's watering already, Carrie," Ernest said.

In the kitchen Marcus watched.

"You look," Carina said, "like a dog waiting to be fed."

He gave a short, loud laugh.

"Or perhaps you're doing a time and motion study on me." She pushed the corner of a newspaper towards him and took the pen from his top pocket. "Record your findings with this."

He snatched back his pen and her hand with it. "That,

136

Miss Ascott, was blatant theft. Not to mention the most colossal piece of impertinence."

"It wasn't theft, Mr. de Verrier," she smiled at him cheekily, "because I'm returning it to you at once. And it wasn't impertinence because –" she caught the look in his eyes, "because –" Her voice tailed off and she indicated that she wanted her hand back. He gave it back.

They had the meal in Ernest's small dining-room, with its dark oak overmantel and its grained and varnished woodwork. The carpet was worn, the mahogany sideboard large and a relic from the family life of the past. Under the curtained window a dark green chenille tablecloth covered a circular table on which stood a leafy pot plant. The room could not have been more different from the opulent and airy spaciousness of the Ascott home, but Carina delighted in the difference. She felt that here, she fitted in. She really belonged.

"So the poor little rich girl can cook?"

The sarcastic question sliced like a carving knife into her ease of mind. Once again she was the sacrificial offering on the altar of his deep-rooted prejudices. He smiled at the frown he had brought to her face.

"Don't keep calling her that, Marcus," Ernest said. "It grates."

"It's all right, Mr. de Verrier," Carina remarked, forcing herself to sound casual, "Marcus's bias against me is so strong that if my skin were a different colour it would be called racial prejudice, and if it were any of my beliefs he was constantly attacking, it would be called religious intolerance. If it were one or the other, I could argue with him openly on an intellectual plane. As it is, I have no basis for argument. And I have no redress."

Marcus paled slightly, shot her an odd glance and with his finger traced the pattern on the tablecloth. "*Touché*," he said.

Ernest slapped his thigh under the table. "I warned you, lad, when our Carrie's provoked, she bites."

"Please accept my apologies, Carina," Marcus said quietly. He gave a strained smile. "You have sharp teeth."

At her singing lesson the following week, Marcus asked if she and her friends were taking their weekly walk in the forest next day.

"Yes," she told him, her hopes rising in a blaze of fire like a rocket heading for outer space. "Are you coming with us?"

"I might," he said with a vague smile.

He did. His mood when he joined them was buoyant. Once again he was swamped by the crowd, but after tolerating the crush for a few moments, he pushed his way through them like a swimmer battling against the current. He reached Carina's side and flung his arm across her shoulders as if she were a life raft and his only hope of survival.

"I made it," he said, looking into her face. "Glad I did?"

"I think so." He shook her shoulder a little at her prevarication. She could not tell him that her heart felt as if it were weightless like a man inside a space capsule.

Seth walked beside Carina and Marcus for most of the way. He looked a little sulky, and glanced at them from time to time as if wondering what might be going on between them. He said pointedly,

"I miss you, Carina. Since you stopped working with me, I haven't got myself another partner." He shot an assessing look at Marcus, and went on, pressing his point, "No one else can seem to match the right words to my music like you did." He laughed, but it was a negative sound. "Did you have to let Marcus coerce you away from the folk idiom and the protest music we specialised in? You often used to say how much you loved it, yet look how willingly you left it behind."

He glanced at Carina this time to see how much his words were affecting her. She looked a little embarrassed and was staring at the ground. Marcus was, too.

Seth persisted, "Still got your guitar, Carina?"

"Well, I –" She and Marcus exchanged glances and the message which flashed between them seemed to catch Seth on the raw. He pulled in his lips. "Unfortunately," Carina went on, "it's broken. Marcus's father tried to mend it, but no go."

"Didn't know you knew Marcus's father." The remark was greeted with silence, which seemed to incense him even more. "Why don't you buy another? You could afford it. I can't imagine you without one for long. Life surely can't be worth living for you without a guitar to nurse."

Again Carina looked at Marcus, as if for guidance.

With a touch of malice Seth said, "I've got a spare one you can have. You could borrow it for as long as you liked." He gave her a sly look. "When we go to the old people's clubs they always ask about you. I think they feel you've let them down."

He saw with satisfaction how his words had made her squirm. He grinned to himself as he saw her try to throw off Marcus's arm as if it were a yoke weighing her down and restricting her movements.

Marcus took the hint immediately. He removed his arm and pushed his hands deep into his pockets. He was frowning and it was his turn to draw in his lips. He said at last, and although his voice was controlled, it contained an unmistakable hint of anger, "Sorry to disappoint the others – and you, Seth – but I'm not letting this girl escape from me now. I'm not prepared to allow the beautiful voice she possesses to be lost to the world."

His arm went back to her shoulders and with a proprietorial action pulled her against him. The move shut Seth out so effectively he had no choice but to leave them alone. He walked on to join the others.

Carina did not speak because all her thoughts had been placed under a strict censorship. Any words which might have come from her at that moment would have given away

139

her happiness. She did not question Marcus's motives. Instead she took with gratitude whatever he cared to offer in the way of friendship – her natural pessimism would allow it to be nothing more – even if the offering came in the form of an arm flung carelessly round her shoulders, or a box of chocolates to be shared with others.

So she turned a silent, radiant face to his, and she did not realise that her expression was like an open book with all the words in large print.

They sat together at tea and walked back, hands linked, falling behind the others until they were out of sight. Seth had given up. He had conceded victory to Marcus.

The kiss had been inevitable from the start. It happened about half-way home. Her lips were warm and responsive and Marcus drank deeply like a traveller at an oasis who, in crossing the desert, had used up his store of water too soon.

There crept into her mind a question which gave a taste of bitterness to his lingering lips. Was he using her merely as a weapon with which to purge himself of the humiliating rejection in the past by a girl who had been so similar to herself in both background and upbringing? Was he exploiting this infatuation he alleged she had for him by binding her to him more securely, thus making sure that the voice he was helping to create – her voice – was not, as he had put it to Seth, lost to the world?

But whatever the answers to these questions might be, her response to his second kiss broke through the barrier of restraint she had imposed on herself and escaped her control entirely. It was not the response of an infatuated girl, but of a woman in love, desperately so. Desperate because she knew that whatever her feelings for him might be, he would never, come what may, allow himself to be in love with her.

She could not take him home, she was thinking, as other girls could take the men they loved. "Home" meant patronage and condescension and the lady-of-the-manor smile, and Marcus of all people would not stand for that.

They walked on, arms round each other, and when Marcus tried to kiss her again, she held him off. Feeling her resistance, he gripped her shoulders. "What's the matter?" he demanded, but it was impossible to tell him. He looked into the large eyes gazing up at him and saw the integrity and uncertainty she could not hide, but he seemed to find no answer to his question. They walked on in silence, he frowning, she surprisingly near to tears.

This feeling between them – whatever it was – had no future. She knew that however much he might pretend, however much he might fool himself, he would never entirely trust her. Always there would be the barrier of her background which he despised, and her parents, on whom he looked with contempt. In their darker moments – all relationships had those – the barrier would be there like a mound of mud for him to throw in her face and blind her.

The problem stayed unresolved in her mind, but they spent the evening happily enough, talking music and holding hands, while Ernest looked on without surprise, full of smiles, approval – and apprehension.

During working hours their behaviour was impeccable. They kept their secret steadfastly. Even Faith Ringstead did not seem to suspect. At Carina's singing lessons Marcus did not touch her. He was friendly and encouraging, but his manner was rigidly detached. He was all teacher.

At Ernest's house they abandoned the restraint they had imposed on themselves by day and behaved like any young couple with marriage in mind. But underneath all her happiness, Carina began to despair. She did not have marriage in mind because she was convinced that Marcus did not have it in mind. Even if he had, she told herself, it could never be. If, as a result of his love for her – *did* he love her? He had never said so – he had pushed his prejudices against her to the back of his thoughts, it could only be a temporary gesture. They were lying in the darkness of his mind,

141

spawning and multiplying, waiting for the most propitious moment to rise to the surface and do their worst.

It was April now. Carina was out every evening, either at Ernest's house or walking in the forest with Marcus. The trees were alight with the delicate green of spring, the bird-song, like a canopy of sound overhead reflected back the couple's pleasure in each other.

But always there was a barrier between them. Always, whenever Marcus came too near to the limits which she had imposed on their relationship, she drew away from him, leaving him deserted and solitary.

It was a barrier, a withdrawal which puzzled – and frightened – Carina herself. Is it because of how I'm made? she wondered. Marcus had once asked, "Are you frigid, Carina?" The answer, as the days passed, seemed to be becoming more and more apparent. It would, she was sure, be "yes".

The day of the second concert of the session arrived. Marcus had coached Carina to the limit of her ability. It was a limit, he had discovered, which could be stretched progressively further as the weeks had passed.

Fleur Leeson had kept her promise and was coming to the concert. When it was over, Marcus was taking Fleur out to dinner. Carina's mother had surprisingly consented to buy a ticket, but whether she would actually *come*, she had said, depended upon her other commitments.

Ernest would, of course, be in the audience, and whether her mother was there or not, Carina knew she would sing to him.

She was suffering badly from nerves. Her future could depend on her performance that evening. She would be singing songs by Brahms and the aria *Love and Music* from Puccini's *Tosca*. She had analysed the scores painstakingly with Marcus, studying the accompaniment on his insistence because, he said, it would make her into not just a singer, but a complete artist.

142

It would be so different this time. Not only were she and Marcus, who was accompanying her, in complete accord, but their teamwork came through and wove itself into the fabric of her singing.

As she stood on the platform, hands loosely linked, the faces below became a blur, an uplifted mass, each one indistinguishable from the other. But one she pinpointed at once – Ernest, near the back, to whom she projected her voice and directed her message. She did not know, until the end of her performance, when the blurred images cleared, whether her mother was there.

But Phyllis had come after all. She was sitting in the front row and there was a strange pride in her eyes as she gazed up at her "black-haired beauty" of a daughter. Carina, accepting the applause with the graciousness she had acquired as the months had passed, felt a spurt of something very close to filial tenderness at her mother's pleasure in her performance.

Afterwards, when the concert was over, Carina expected her mother to seek her out, but Ernest, who had come backstage in search of his grandson, told her that Phyllis, whom he had met once while waiting in the sports car outside the Ascott home, had left the hall immediately after Carina's performance had ended.

Ernest looked round for a chair and Carina gave him one. He sat beside her as she waited for the verdict of the guest of honour. She thought he looked tired. It occurred to her that he had been looking frail for some time and it worried her. He told her that her singing had been better than ever. "You got an ovation, Carrie, and you deserved it."

She shrugged, too modest to accept his praise. "Marcus said these audiences would applaud anyone, however bad they were, because they are the 'mums and dads' of the performers."

"Don't underrate yourself, Carina." She swung round to find Marcus behind her. Fleur Leeson was with him.

143

"I was most impressed, Miss Ascott," Fleur said. "I think Marcus has a winner in you. I told you I trusted his judgement. I also told him I thought I might be able to get you accepted by the promoters of a concert scheduled to take place in a month or so in London. They specialise in giving young performers a chance to prove their worth, but of course they are required to have reached a certain high standard before they can be considered. I believe you've reached it. How would you like that?"

"Marcus?" Carina looked for him for reassurance, for the right answer.

"We should be delighted to have such a chance, wouldn't we, Carina?"

She noticed with joy his use of the plural. "We". Marcus would be with her. "It would be wonderful," she said, "that is, if you really think I could rise to it."

"No doubt about that." Fleur patted her arm. "With the right teaching – which you have – and the right encouragement, you could be on your way to great things in a year or two. It will be hard work, Miss Ascott, but take it from me – and I've been through it – it will be worth it."

Carina asked her mother that evening how she had enjoyed the concert. Phyllis looked at her, as if striving to remember what her daughter was talking about. "Oh, the concert. Well, I only went to hear you, and you were wonderful, darling, wonderful . . ." Her voice tailed off vaguely as if the whole episode had already receded to the back of her mind, had taken its rightful place amongst all the other compulsory attendances which she made as a local member of sundry guilds and committees. "Of course," she rallied brightly, "we always have encouraged you, your father and I. We bought you the piano, didn't we, and your stereo equipment, and we had the den built, and –"

"Yes, Mother," said Carina flatly, "you certainly have given me a lot of things." But, she wanted to add, encouragement? Loving interest in my activities? Affectionate support as well as material aids? Never.

She went to bed deflated instead of elated, wishing she had spent the evening with Ernest, discussing the concert and hearing him talk of his pride in her achievements. She wished she could phone Marcus – any contact with him would have sufficed – but she knew he was out, dining with Fleur Leeson at the most expensive hotel in the town.

"Where are you going, Carina?" It was a few evenings later. Dinner was over and Lloyd stood as Carina stood. The swift action of his neat, nimble body in its immaculate suit was a challenge in itself. Usually a man who calculated to the last detail his every movement, and which to some people made him appear to be rather slow, his rapid matching of her rising to her feet was a gesture which put Carina on her guard. It was plain she was coming to the end of the rope they had allowed her to have. The questions had begun.

"To Mr. de Verrier's."

"The old man?" She nodded. "I don't approve of your continued friendship with him. Incidentally," he frowned and spoke slowly as if in the act of remembering, "isn't de Verrier the name of the man you brought here once? Something to do with the school of music? A teacher?"

"Marcus de Verrier is the head of the school. He is also Mr. de Verrier's grandson and they share the same house. I told you so when he first arrived in the district, but you took no notice."

"And isn't he the man who teaches you singing? Ah, now I see the attraction." He followed her to the door.

She had to put him off the scent. "If Marcus de Verrier happens to live with his grandfather, Ernest de Verrier, there's nothing I can do about it, is there?"

For a moment her father looked stumped. Was it stalemate?

"Every evening is a lot of times to go and see an old man, Carina. There must be another reason why a young

145

girl like you goes to see a man in his dotage and nearing the end of his life span."

"No, he's not," she wanted to cry, "he's got years and years yet."

He watched her slow, revealing flush and the fear darkening her eyes. "There is another reason, isn't there?" Checkmate, his smile said. You've lost. "I will not have you mixing with undesirable people, Carina."

"They're *not* undesirable!"

"They are not in our class."

"Marcus is not in our intellectual class. He's way above us." Clearly her father did not like that. "He's a musician –"

"And how much do musicians earn? Tell me that."

Did he have to measure everything in terms of currency?

"He's not *that* sort of musician. He's a teacher –"

Her father asked coldly, "And how much do teachers earn?"

"Oh, for goodness' sake! He's not really a teacher, either . . ." This was getting nowhere, she was chasing her tail like a gyrating dog. "Anyway, it's no concern of mine – or yours – how much he earns. He hasn't proposed to me. In fact, I'm sure he has no intention . . ." She stopped, horrified at the construction her father might put upon that.

She turned and ran, out of the front door and into her car. She pulled up with a screech of brakes outside Ernest's house. She hurtled up the garden path, but even so Marcus was there to let her in.

"Only you could arrive with such an ear-splitting fanfare. How you do maltreat your car's inside. It's oddly out of character for you to be such a reckless driver."

She burst out, "You call *me* a reckless driver? You accuse me, of all people . . ." But of course he didn't know. How could he, when she had never told him about the road accident that had turned her into an orphan? "It's just that I'm in a temper, a foul temper. So –" she looked so threat-

146

ening he laughed, "so keep your distance if you want to remain in one piece."

"Keep my distance? If that's not an invitation . . ."

He took her into his arms with gentleness because, despite her half-comical outburst, he had sensed she was profoundly disturbed. As he kissed her, she tried to pull away, but with a suddenness which startled him, she clung like someone in a rough sea clinging to an overturned boat with slipping fingers . . .

They stood for a few moments, she trying to draw strength from his strength, he deeply moved, and concerned, by her apparent need of him.

"Come on, Marcus," Ernest called, "let her come and see me. You can whisper sweet nothings later on."

Marcus looked down at her. "Carina?" She detached herself from him and apologised. He said, "Tell me what's wrong?"

"I can't."

Ernest said, "Hallo, Carrie." He pulled himself to the front of the armchair. "What's wrong, lass? Tell Ernest," as if he were addressing a child, "tell the old man."

"I can't, Mr. de Verrier," she whispered. For the first time in their acquaintance, she had to keep a secret from him, he who knew all her secrets. She could not tell even him what her father had said about the de Verriers.

Ernest relaxed to the back of his chair. "Cheer her up, Marcus. Play back the tape you made of her singing at the concert."

She looked up, her spirits lifting at once. "Did you record it?"

"One of the students did it for me. Listen carefully, Carina, listen critically and learn by any mistakes you think you made. We'll talk it over later."

Her voice filled the small room, the voice which, with its purity and perfection of tone, astonished her every time she heard a playback of it. Ernest closed his eyes, Marcus sat forward in his chair, hands clasped loosely. Carina hugged

147

a bent, trousered knee and tried to obey Marcus's instructions.

When the recording had ended, Marcus said, "What's your verdict?"

"Well," tentatively, "I've improved, haven't I?"

"My word, you've improved!"

"I told you she was modest, Marcus," Ernest said.

"A little more self-assurance wouldn't go amiss," Marcus commented. "One thing a successful singer must have is belief in herself. Now comes the reckoning, Carina. I shall analyse that voice, I shall criticise it, always constructively, I hope, and I hope too that you'll learn from what I have to say – and not take umbrage as you did last time! Promise?"

"I promise."

So he pointed out her faults, and her virtues, suggesting that here and there she should have put more emotion into her singing, reasoned, controlled emotion, not emotion run riot. "Here," he said, "you were not listening to yourself, there you were not letting the music flow through your mind before it came through your lips." He pulled her up and held her hands. "But it's there, Carina, that potential. One day you'll be a force in the musical world to be reckoned with, I promise you that."

"And," said Ernest, his eyes lighting up as he looked into the future, Carina's future, "I'll be there to see it happen, lass. You can count on me. I won't let you down."

Carina and Marcus were walking in the forest. It was warm and the late evening sun streamed in dazzling golden diagonal rays through the trees, making shadow patterns on the ground and turning the trunks and branches into shapes without substance.

They sat down and there was no dampness beneath them, because the ground was dry through lack of rain. He leaned over her and pushed her down to lie full-length, then he tugged her against him and they were locked together by his gripping arms.

For a long moment they lay in silence, becoming one with the sounds and scents of the forest. The sun moved towards its setting and the shadows lengthened and all the creatures of the forest seemed to know that darkness was not far away.

Marcus's head came down, blotting out the fading daylight, and as his exploring mouth found hers at last, Carina knew that no matter how close they pressed they would not get near to each other. Always, at a certain moment, she would withdraw. It had happened many times before, and she would be no different now.

Even as they made love, she had a searing, terrifying premonition that this desperate, wonderful thing between them would, by some means, be destroyed. Marcus touched her and caressed her and she found herself responding with a wild, frightening abandon. He seemed overjoyed and murmured endearments. His hands and lips became more persuasive and more demanding – and a door was slammed in his face.

She caught at his wrists and held them still. "No, Marcus, no," she whispered.

It came to her like a lightning flash lighting up the landscape that now she knew the reason for her sudden inexplicable withdrawals, her apparent frigidity. It was not frigidity at all, it was the sum of her experiences since childhood, when her world lay in ruins at her feet.

Stop the future now, she wanted to cry. No child of mine will ever suffer what I suffered, a branch torn from a parent tree, rootless, belonging to no one but myself. No child of mine will ever be deprived of what I was deprived – the love of its mother – *and* its father . . .

"Sorry, my sweet," Marcus whispered, "you're right, of course, you're quite right."

He rolled on to his back, the twigs crackling with the

149

movement of his body. He put an arm across his eyes and might have been asleep. Carina lay still beside him. The sun had almost gone and the birds, sensing the imminence of darkness, twittered and called with a touch of desperation, as if there was barely time to finish their song before nightfall.

"I'll go home with you, Carina." The words hung and hovered, mingling with the breeze stirring the branches. The air, deprived of the sun's warmth, turned chill. Carina shivered.

Marcus turned on his side towards her and rested on his elbow, smoothing back her hair and touching her closed eyes. "You know why, don't you? We can't go on like this."

She took his hand and moved it, palm open, against her cheek. "Marcus, oh, Marcus," she whispered. She was terrified.

They kissed as they approached the house. Marcus turned her face and put his lips to hers. It seemed to be a calculated action on his part, an intimation – and a warning – to whoever might be watching.

The front door was opened to them immediately and Carina knew there had been a witness to the kiss.

Phyllis said, the patronage in her face merging with the delicately applied make-up and becoming part of it, "Darling, you've brought that Mr. de Verri-ay home with you again." She raised ingenuous yet challenging eyes to Marcus and waited for the correction. None came.

Marcus lifted the corners of his mouth in the semblance of a smile. His arm settled more surely round Carina's waist and he said, "I persuaded her, Mrs. Ascott. I wanted to see you."

A frown corrugated the skin between the eyes, which were sincerely troubled, the breath was caught and held. The word "oh" was released slowly from her throat and in the sound was a wealth of meaning, an immediate grasping of the situation and a total rejection of what was to come.

"Where's Father?" Carina asked.

150

"In the morning room, dear, working." It was a small room leading off the hall, and Lloyd used it as an office.

"Is it possible to see him, Mrs. Ascott?" Marcus asked, his manner polite and as civil as he could manage to make it.

"I – er – well, I – er –" Phyllis was uncharacteristically at an utter loss. Not many situations were beyond her manipulation, but this one seemed to be. And at all costs, her uneasy expression said, this particular situation must be dealt with speedily, positively and conclusively. For this she needed support and she knew where she would find it.

"Take Mr. de Verri–ay into the drawing-room, Carina. I'll – er –" she eyed Marcus doubtfully, "I'll go and see my husband, Mr. – er – de Verri-ay. He's rather busy, you know."

"The matter is of some importance, Mrs. Ascott." Marcus's tone was correct and courteous, but even with his iron control he seemed unable to keep a touch of rebuke out of it.

Phyllis disappeared and the long wait began. Marcus wandered round the room, restless, withdrawn, his impatience growing with every minute that passed. Carina switched on the wall lights and drew the heavy blue velvet curtains across the floor to ceiling windows. He watched, chinking the money in his pockets.

She went to his side. "Marcus?" He saw the fear in her eyes and turned from it. She was asking him for comfort, but at that moment he seemed to have none to give. He stared savagely round him. To Carina's distressed eyes it looked as though the luxury in which she lived every day of her life filled him with a revulsion which almost sickened him. She knew in a moment of truth that no matter how hard he tried, he would never reconcile himself to it.

It was plain that he was re-living the past. By his restlessness, his frown, his look of simmering anger, it seemed that he was already regretting his decision to come, to bring matters to a head, to do the right thing and propose marriage. "I have been here before," his eyes said.

"The old technique," he muttered viciously, "keep them waiting, wear down their confidence, get them shaking in their shoes, then give them the interview they asked for." He roved about. "Why in God's name did I come? Did I have to put my head in a noose – the same noose – only to have it pulled tight again until I choked?" He seemed only half aware that he was talking aloud. Now the anger in his eyes included Carina, and she shrank from it.

"Marcus?" It was a frightened whimper, like a child afraid of the dark. She could feel him going away from her, melting into nothingness like a figure in a dream, without substance like those trees in the forest as darkness approached. She thought if she tried to touch him, there would be nothing there, not even shadow.

She touched his arm and he was there. She turned up her face, white with anxiety, and he saw her glowing eyes, with that sadness and uncertainty in them which could not be explained but which was moving beyond words.

His arms wrapped about her and as they kissed, their passion and desire rekindled. Yet Carina felt it was also a kiss of farewell, because how could his love – was it love? He had never once mentioned the word – stand up to what she was sure was to come. Even now she could feel brutality creeping into his kiss, as though he was already classifying her with her parents and treating her with the contempt with which he treated them.

Her mother called and Carina drew herself from his arms and went to find her. Marcus followed. Phyllis was in the morning room with her husband. Carina joined them while Marcus lingered outside in the hall.

Lloyd asked, his voice belligerent and loud, "What has that man de Verri-ay come to see me for? I can think of no possible reason, unless it's to persuade me to give him a job."

The insult curdled in the air like milk standing too long in the sun.

"He doesn't need a job, Father," Carina answered
152

patiently – it was essential to humour him. "He already has one. It's because we're – I'm – we're in love."

"Is that all? Then why the hell must he come running to me to tell me that?"

Carina floundered, bewildered by her father's tone. He had out-manoeuvred her. She simply did not know how to deal with the situation.

"He's after your money," Lloyd rapped out. "If he wants a loan, tell him I'll give him one on the usual terms. But he's not going to get you thrown in as a bonus."

Carina unclenched her fists and put her hand to her head. She knew Marcus could hear every word.

"Darling," Phyllis said, "he's only a struggling musician, almost a pauper compared with us. We want a better match for you than that. The money we give you as a monthly allowance is probably as much if not more than he earns in the same length of time. You know how poorly paid teachers are."

Lloyd shuffled the papers in front of him, closing the conversation. "I'm too busy to see the fellow. Tell him to go whining to someone else for money, because that's what he wants, not you – the girl – but the money that goes with you."

"*Father!*" she shrieked, like an animal caught in a cunningly placed trap, "he's not like that, he's –"

Phyllis interrupted, her voice coaxing, "Have fun with him, if you like, darling, but for heaven's sake, don't take him seriously. You can't *marry* the man, it's out of the question."

"*Have fun with him.*" The voice from the past must have taunted Marcus's ears.

He pushed open the morning-room door. He was white and seemed to be gripped by a searing, blazing anger. But when he spoke, his tone was icy cold. "For the record, Mrs. Ascott, I am not a pauper, I am not a half-starved teacher, nor am I a 'struggling musician', as you rather quaintly put it. My salary is good – good enough to support a wife of reasonable, *moderate* tastes," his eyes rested contemptuously on Carina, "plus a family, if I so desired. But the money I earn would, no doubt, in your and your husband's eyes be considered mere pocket money."

No one stirred. It was as if he were speaking to three statues.

"I have no intention of trying to talk my way into being admitted into this family as a son-in-law." Carina made an agitated movement, but it was ignored. "I know my 'application' would be turned down. I don't come out of the 'top drawer', either socially or genealogically. I have no noble forebears, no aristocratic ancestors to wave tantalisingly in front of your noses with which to enhance my desirability and my chances of acceptance.

"I have only honesty and integrity to offer as family assets — assets I regard as qualities beyond price, but which you and your husband no doubt rate far lower than the wealth and material possessions which you both insist any prospective son-in-law of yours must have. So you may stop worrying here and now. Your daughter is quite safe from my clutches. When I've gone, you can breathe a sigh of relief. You will not see me here again."

He turned to go, but Carina threw herself in his path. She clutched his arm, and shrieked, "Take me with you, Marcus!" but he put his hands on her shoulders and swung her out of the way. The front door opened and closed. Then there was silence.

CHAPTER EIGHT

CARINA lay spent on her bed. Her energy had drained out of her body with the tears. The end of an interlude, she thought. No more Marcus, except in the formal atmosphere of the singing lessons. No more running to him, clinging to him, feeling his strength, of mind as well as body. He could only hate her after this.

Perhaps she could leave home. But with her father's allowance no longer behind her, she could not survive. She had no skills, she could not type or do office work, had no artistic ability. What sort of job could she do without experience, without training? Shop assistant? Perhaps. But she would not earn much doing that, not enough to pay rent and eat and clothe herself.

Marcus was right. She had lived such a sheltered life, had been so conditioned by her upbringing and the luxury of her background, she would be as helpless as a newborn kitten in the big outside world.

With little interest she opened Justine's letter which had been waiting for her since morning. "Avery came to see me," Justine had written. "Fancy him flying all this way especially to see little me! Guess what, I'm giving him a go. I've got his ring – on third finger, left hand. It looks good there. We can have some fun together. If I can't find anyone else, I might even marry him. After all, it's not for life these days, is it?" Carina, shocked, thought, what about the children? But knowing Justine, she was certain she would take good care that there were not any children until she was ready to have them.

"I asked Avery," the letter went on, "what had happened between you two. He told me and I laughed and laughed. I said he was a fool to let the fact that you were adopted worry him, because you probably came of better parental stock than I did! That shook him, temporarily. He soon recovered, though, when he remembered all the money in the family. I suppose he thinks it more than makes up for any 'bad blood' I might have inherited from the Ascott ancestors!"

Thank goodness, Carina thought, folding the letter, that there could now be no suggestion that she and Avery might come together again.

Faith Ringstead was back in favour. Marcus de Verrier was taking her out again. They were often seen together during working hours or driving away in Marcus's car at the end of the day.

Faith wore the rapturous smile of one who had landed a top job in competition against a horde of less fortunate applicants. Did Marcus, Carina wondered, kiss her? Did he make love to her as passionately as he had made love to her, Carina, in happier days? The thought of it, of even a kiss exchanged between those two, gave Carina a feeling of horror, like someone afraid of heights standing on the edge of a cliff and seeing the beach hundreds of feet below.

But whether Marcus was with Faith or not, he did not spare even as much as a single glance for Carina.

A woman teacher was waiting for her when she attended her next singing lesson. She was a part-time teacher, she explained, and her name was Mrs. Stanley.

"Mr. de Verrier has told me of your progress, dear, and that you have an important concert coming along in London. Now, if you could tell me what you've done to date?"

Accepting the inevitable, wearily, miserably, Carina told

her. The singing lesson was a failure. "Never mind," said Mrs. Stanley cheerfully, "it's probably only because we haven't got used to each other yet."

"I'm sorry," Carina said, "I must be off form. Did Mr. de Verrier say why he was handing me over to you?"

"He said he was too busy, much too busy to give you any more instruction. But, off form or not, I can hear you have a good voice, so it won't be long before we both adapt to each other."

But, Carina thought, the whole meaning had gone out of life. There was little point now in continuing at the school of music.

One evening Carina called on Ernest. He asked bluntly, "What's happened between you and Marcus? I tried to get it out of him, but he just stalked upstairs."

She sat on the footstool, her head drooping, miserable beyond tears, and told Ernest everything. He shook his head. "It's history repeating itself, Carrie. After the first lot he vowed never again, but it did happen again, and now you're bearing the brunt. Can't you talk him round, lass?"

"I can't get near him, Mr. de Verrier. He won't even look at me unless he has to." She said in a whisper, "I don't know how much longer I can stand it. It's terrible passing him in the corridor and having him treat me as though I were a stranger."

Ernest heard the waver and knew she was on the brink of tears. He couldn't bear to hear her cry. He pulled himself out of his chair, taking every movement slowly, as if his mind were instructing his limbs as to what to do next. He opened the door to the hall, raised his voice and shouted, "Marcus!"

A door opened and there was an answering, "Yes?"

"Come down, lad."

"Sorry, can't spare the time. I'm busy."

"You're not so busy you can't spare a few minutes for your old grandfather." He walked back to his chair. "He'll come."

And Marcus did come, reluctantly entering the room, staring at the drooping head and the bent back that was turned to him. "Well, Grandfather, what do you want me for?"

"Come and make it up with this girl."

He stiffened. "Sorry. Nothing doing."

"I told you," came from the mass of black hair that had fallen over Carina's face, "I'm not my parents' keeper. I'm not responsible for how they act. You can't lay the blame for their insults and their treatment of you at my door."

There was a deep silence. Then, "Look, Carina," he walked across to stand in front of her, "in my – friendship with you, I realise now that I was living in a fool's paradise. I was deliberately closing my eyes to the glaring facts. I know you're past the age of parents' consent, but you simply do not know how disastrous an effect the lack of it can have on a couple's relationship. But parental approval apart, one has only to look at you to see how impossible it would be for any man of moderate means to keep up with your tastes."

"But, Marcus," she pleaded, then stopped, knowing her case was a hopeless one. Couldn't he see that she only wore the clothes and the jewellery because they were there? She tossed back her hair and looked up at him. The brown, honest, puzzling eyes met his and he seemed to make a superhuman effort to overcome the pull of them. He succeeded and the look he returned to her was all the more hard and intractable for the momentary vacillation that preceded it.

"What do you want me to do, Marcus?" she pleaded. "Dress in sackcloth and rags, go about without shoes, half-starved, and live in a hovel just to pander to your upside down sense of values? Would you like me any better – I can't say 'love' because I know now you've never loved me – if I denied myself all the luxuries that come my way, never played that beautiful piano I was given, never used that stereo equipment I was given, never wore the lovely clothes in my wardrobe?" Her voice wavered again, but she had it under control immediately. "I could do without the whole damned lot, I could live quite happily without every single one, if I – if you – if we . . ."

"Carina," his voice held no tenderness, no compassion, "stop fooling yourself. You may think you can do without all those things, you might even manage it for a time, but you've been so conditioned to your way of life, you would soon become restless. You would start resenting the comparative poverty of the environment you had moved into, longing for all you had left behind. You would start thinking of your parents, wanting to see them, wishing you hadn't broken away – and hating the man who had made you." He ignored the violent shake of her head. "If a baby came you would want to show it off to the family, you'd want their blessing. It's only natural. It wouldn't work, Carina, it simply would not work."

Her eyes filled and she shook her head again, but she was forced to acknowledge defeat. She could not go on pleading her case and court humiliation and dismissal at his hands. She covered her face, her heart was breaking, but Marcus could not hear it. How could he when it made no sound?

"You're misjudging her, Marcus." The old man's voice held a warning. "You don't know how badly, grandson. Carina, can't I tell –"

She raised her head. "No, no, *no*! What good would it do?" Her lip trembled. "Oh, go away," she sobbed to Marcus, "go *away*!"

And Marcus went away.

The singing lessons continued to misfire. Mrs. Stanley said she was getting quite worried.

"You'll have to come back on form soon, dear, otherwise I shall have to suggest to Mr. de Verrier that your appearance at the London concert be cancelled." Seeing the stricken look on the girl's face she said sympathetically, "Never mind, there's always another time. Better to postpone it and wait until you're really ready than go ahead and make a mess of it. Such a wonderful chance for a young girl! Perhaps if you were to practise more, dear . . .?"

So practise Carina did. That evening she returned to the school and found an empty room. She did a few vocal exercises, but there seemed to be a constriction in her throat. She went on to some songs, flipping through the music scores, trying to find one she liked singing. *Ich Liebe Dich?* No, no! *On Wings of Song?* Perhaps.

She played the accompaniment and started to sing. It was a choked, inhibited effort and it appalled her. What had happened to her voice? It had gone, leaving a mockery of sound behind. She tried again, desperate now, putting into effect all that Marcus had taught her, but it was no use.

She raised her fists and banged them over the keys, making a jangling, jarring noise, then she held her head with both hands.

The door opened. "What in heaven's name –?" Marcus said, then, "Oh, it's you. I might have guessed. What are you doing here?"

She stood up, pale, shaking. "Marcus, my voice – it's gone. I can't sing any more. I open my mouth and all that comes out is a noise, a shocking noise."

He closed the door. "Don't be a fool, Carina. Of course you can sing."

She shook her head. "Not any more. There's something wrong." She looked about her as if she had never seen the room before. "I know what it is. I told you a long time ago. It's the atmosphere. I can't sing in an unsympathetic atmosphere."

"Good God, Carina, a singer is a singer, whatever the 'atmosphere', whether she's on a mountain top or the bottom of a well."

She stared at him. "I tell you, it's no good. Ever since you gave up teaching me, something's gone wrong."

"What are you trying to say – that it's my fault?"

160

"I told you before that you motivated me. Now I've lost all incentive. And my voice with it."

He looked suspicious. "Is this your way of trying to inveigle me back into teaching you?"

"Do you really mistrust me so much you believe me capable of such devious tactics?"

"I beg your pardon." Even his apology mocked her. "An Ascott is, of course, always above suspicion." He looked at her, seeing her misery dragging down her shoulders, and his manner softened a little. He went towards her, stretching out his hand to take hers, but she shrank away from him. His eyes narrowed angrily, and he bit out, "If your voice doesn't recover in time we shall just have to cancel your performance at the concert."

"But, Marcus –" She could not believe that he could be so callous. "Don't you *care* any more?"

His body went slack and it was only then that she noticed the shadows around his eyes. "I suppose I shall have to care. We must not cancel your appearance if it can possibly be avoided. I shall have to have a word with Mrs. Stanley." There was a marked lack of interest in his voice, and it seemed he was dismissing her.

She gathered up the music and went to the door.

"Where are you going now?"

"Somewhere, anywhere. What's the use of staying here?"

He knew where she was going, of course. How could he fail to guess?

She poured out her heart to Ernest. "But you can't have lost your voice, lass. It must still be there. It's something emotional stopping it, damming it up." He clenched his fist and banged it on the arm of the chair. "My fool of a grandson, can't he see the damage he's doing? Where does he get his pigheadedness from?" He pulled himself forward in the chair, and as he came into the light, it caught at Carina's heart to see how much he had aged lately.

"Are you sure you're well, Mr. de Verrier?"

"Me, well? Of course I'm well, Carrie. I'm good for another twenty years! Look, lass, sing to me like you used to. Pretend you've got a guitar in your hands –"

She jerked upright. "A guitar. That's it! Seth said he'd lend me one." She ran to the door. "I'll be back, Mr. de Verrier, I won't be long."

But she was longer than she thought she would be. Seth pulled her inside the house. "The long-lost girl-friend returns. Now I've got you here, you're not running away. Come and listen to my new piece, then think of some words." He pushed her into the dining-room and put a guitar into her hands. "Listen to this, and get your brain going."

He played his music two or three times and she picked it out on the guitar. She started humming, and words came into her mind. *"It's tomorrow we must work for. What's the use of yesterday? Today is nearly over, but tomorrow's inside today."*

Seth made a beckoning motion. "Come on, give some more."

She sang, *"The sun will rise tomorrow, Even if we've moved on. Tomorrow's the thing to work for, Because today has almost gone."*

Seth thrust a pencil and paper in her hand. "Write them down."

"They'll need polishing," she said. "Won't do as they stand."

"We'll work on them, Carina, when you come again. While you're here, let's run through our others."

So Carina sang, while Seth played, *Think of a life* and *The conscience of the world.* Then Carina sang, and sang again.

"I can sing, Seth!" she cried. *"I can sing!"*

"Who said you couldn't?" Seth asked absentmindedly. He had gone back to working on their new song.

She held out his guitar. "May I borrow this?"

162

"I said you could, didn't I? But only if you promise to come again."

"I promise, Seth, I promise." Her voice faded as she ran out to her car.

She sank down breathless on the footstool in front of Ernest, and like a child finding a lost toy, she looked at the guitar, turned it over and played it with loving, stroking hands.

At Ernest's request she ran through her old repertoire, *Songs my mother taught me, Plaisir d'Amour*, and everything else he asked her to sing.

They did not hear Marcus open the door. He said, stiff with anger, "What the hell are you doing with that guitar?"

She swung round, her face ecstatic. "I can sing again, Marcus, my voice has come back."

"Don't be angry with her, Marcus," Ernest pleaded. "It's the guitar that's done the trick. It's undone all the damage you've done."

"Damage I've done? What the blazes does that mean?"

"You know darned well what I mean, grandson." Ernest's voice held a tremor. "Sing to Marcus, Carrie. Come on, Marcus, sit down and listen."

Marcus could not disobey the command. His grandfather seemed in such an emotional state it worried him.

Carina ran her fingers lovingly over the strings and began to sing, her voice full, beautiful and caressingly soft, *Ich Liebe Dich, I love thee, I love thee* ... During the profound silence that followed, she raised brimming eyes to Marcus's. He got up and walked out of the room.

163

CHAPTER NINE

MARCUS took over Carina's singing lessons again. He said that after her histrionics about losing her voice, he had no alternative. She winced at his sarcasm, but let it pass. He was her teacher again and that was all that mattered.

Lloyd asked Carina one evening, "What's this you've been telling your mother about performing at a concert in London?"

She said indifferently that it was in ten days' time. "I haven't mentioned it before because I didn't think you would be interested. In the past you've treated my singing as something of a joke."

"But, darling," Phyllis exclaimed, "how can you *say* that? After giving you that superb piano, after my attending that concert at the music school . . ."

Carina stopped her mother's flow of words by saying she was sorry she had misjudged them, and were they coming to hear her?

"But of course, Carina," her mother said, "how could you think otherwise?"

"How will you get to the concert hall?" Lloyd asked. "You surely aren't intending to drive yourself there?"

"No. I shall have to attend a rehearsal in the afternoon. Marcus de Verrier is taking me."

"So," Lloyd managed to turn the word into a melodramatic threat, "you've taken up with him again, have you?"

"Unfortunately, no," Carina replied calmly. "You've killed all that. If he has any feeling left for me at all, I think it's turned into hate. He's going because he's my accompanist, and for no other reason."

Lloyd, scarcely bothering to hide his delight at the news, said to his wife, "This calls for a celebration. A new dress, don't you think? We can't have her making her first appearance in London in rags."

Carina suppressed a smile. The description of the beautiful clothes in her wardrobe as "rags" was worthy of Justine, who, it appeared, was truly her father's daughter!

"Well, Carina," Lloyd said heartily, "would you like me to make you a present of an Ascott model gown?"

Carina shrugged. What she wore on the occasion was of little consequence. Such a dress would only widen the gulf which already existed between Marcus and herself. She said ingenuously, "It would be a wonderful advertisement for Ascott clothes, wouldn't it, Father?"

Lloyd, missing the sarcasm and pleased instead with the sudden interest his daughter seemed to be displaying in the family business, agreed wholeheartedly. "We must buy tickets at once. The best seats, of course. I take it there are still tickets available, darling?"

Carina winced. It must have been more than eighteen years since her father had called her that. Which took her back, she calculated swiftly, to just before the birth of Justine.

"Yes, there are still tickets available. Ring the box office."

"I will," said Lloyd, "right now."

The London concert was approaching too fast. Carina was suffering from an acute attack of nerves. They were pulling her muscles as tight as guitar strings. At night doubts tormented her. Was her voice as good as when Fleur Leeson had heard it? Listening to herself as she sang, she felt it was not.

There was something missing, that haunting quality

which Ernest had said had touched the compassion and humanity of her listeners. She panicked, not daring to mention it to Marcus who, in his present unapproachable mood might regard it as a reflection on his teaching ability.

If only he would show even a glimpse of his old warmth and friendliness, she felt it would dislodge the dam, and then the emotion would come flooding through again.

In spite of her resolution not to mention the matter, she burst out one day, "Can't you hear there's something wrong?"

"Wrong? No, there's nothing wrong. Your technique has improved even beyond my expectations." He looked at her reflectively. "Are you throwing a temperament? You're not a prima donna yet, you know."

"My technique? It's not that that's worrying me. I can't feel what I'm singing any more. I'm thinking it as you told me to, but I can't feel it here," she gripped her ribs, "it's coming from my intellect, not my emotions. It's terrible, because there seems to be nothing I can do about it. You're my teacher, Marcus, can't you tell me what to do to make it come from inside?"

He rubbed his hand over his face like a man under severe strain. He tried to deflect her anxiety by making a joke. "I suppose you'll be telling me next you want to take a guitar on to the stage with you in London?"

But the joke misfired. "You don't understand. Not only that," she cried, "you don't care any more. You just don't care!" She ran out, ignoring his command to return.

Now it was only two days to the concert. Faith Ringstead said at the end of a dreary hour-long piano lesson, "So Mr. de Verrier's had to go back to teaching you singing again? He was quite fed up about it. He told me he only did it with the greatest reluctance and because you've been making so much fuss about appearing at that concert in London."

So Marcus had discussed her with Faith. Carina knew by the gloating sound in the woman's voice that she had enjoyed the confidences which, it seemed, Marcus poured into her ear.

"I gather from the things he's let drop that you two just don't hit it off." Faith paused to assess the effect of her words on her listener, noting with malevolent satisfaction the pain on her face. "I know I shouldn't tell you this, but the things he says about you! You know what he calls you?" Carina shook her head dumbly. The blood had drained from her face, and her clasped hands were moist.

"He calls you," Faith went on, running the nail of her thumb over the piano keys and making a clicking sound, "a spoilt little bitch who's had life made a damned sight too easy for you. Isn't he awful, dear?" She did not really expect an answer because she went on immediately, "He said you're as dim as they come and you can't stick at anything for more than a few months and you're as useless as a car without an engine." She stood up to deliver her final fling. "He also said that if he'd had his way he would have thrown you out of the music school at the start and that he can't wait until the end of the session to do just that!"

Faith gathered up the music from the stand and handed a few sheets to Carina. "Isn't the big event the day after tomorrow?" she asked. "Well, good luck. Hope you're in good voice and that you don't let Mr. de Verrier down, after all the trouble he's taken with you." At the door she stopped. "You'll have to put in more time on the piano, Miss Ascott. Your progress seems to have come to a stop lately. You won't pass your exams, you know, if you don't work at it. Don't let this London appearance go to your head, will you, and when it's over think you know it all!"

She swept out, leaving her stupefied pupil staring into space.

Carina could not move. She felt she had been involved in a road accident and that the car in which she had been travelling had been smashed to pieces. She had been thrown clear and had been picked up dazed, bruised and severely

167

shocked. She was alive, but only just. The real injuries were internal, out of sight and out of reach. She would not die of them – not in the accepted sense of the word. But she might as well stop living here and now. She had a feeling of *déjà vu*, of having been there before.

She closed her eyes. And had she once thought Marcus de Verrier might have loved her? Enough, in fact, to want to marry her? Wasn't that why he had asked to see her parents? Or had her father been right and Marcus had been another one after the money and status that would go with her, and when her father had called his bluff, he had cried off?

Her certainty that this theory must be correct brought her to her feet and swept her along the corridor to Marcus's room. By the time she had reached his door, she had worked herself into such a state of anger that even if he had not been alone she would have forced her way in to see him.

But he was alone. His head jerked up from his work and he saw her shock and outrage. "What's the matter, Carina?"

"What's the matter?" she stormed, "I'll tell you what's the matter. Now I know exactly what you think of me, I can't go through with the concert."

He asked slowly, "What do you mean, 'what I think of you'?"

"After what your girl-friend told me you've been saying about me –"

"What girl-friend? I have no girl-friend."

"No? Not Faith Ringstead?"

"And just what have I been saying to Faith Ringstead about you?"

"Terrible things, so awful I want to forget them. I'm not going to sing at the concert, Marcus. I can't, not now . . ." She stopped to control the waver in her voice. "Nothing you can do will make me."

He stood. "There's no backing out, Carina. You promised to appear, and appear you will. You cannot – repeat, cannot – break that promise."

She sank on to a chair. "I'm sorry, I can't face it. Not now, not now . . ." She bent her head and her hair swung forward hiding her tears.

"So," he said quietly, "you're a coward after all. The money you've had behind you all your life has made you soft-centred and weak. It's robbed you of your spirit. What wouldn't other girls, without your advantages, your riches, give for a chance like this, girls who perhaps deserve the lucky break far more than you do?"

"Thanks," she said, drained of animation, "for your bracing, abrasive talk. But it's done nothing for me. It hasn't challenged me, as you no doubt hoped it would. In fact," she walked unsteadily to the door, "it has had the opposite effect. You'd better phone Miss Leeson and ask her if she's free to take my place."

"I'll do no such thing." He hammered on the desk. "Carina, will you come back? Will you listen?"

"I've listened to you enough. It won't do any good listening to you any more. We've come to the end of our journey together, Marcus. I'm getting out and walking. You can drive on without me."

She went straight to Ernest. She had no one else to run to.

He was not in his usual chair. His voice wafted down to her and it sounded feeble. She raced up the stairs and he called out to her to come in. He was in bed, lying back on a mound of pillows, his face white and drawn, his movements slow.

Carina's face turned as pale as Ernest's. "You're ill, Mr. de Verrier." She stood at his bedside and he raised his hand and felt for hers.

"Nothing to worry about, Carrie. Got a chill, rheumatism, stiffness. It catches up with me sometimes."

"But I've never known you ill before, Mr. de Verrier.

169

Have you had the doctor?"

"Yes, Marcus got him to come. Gave me some pills." It seemed an effort for him to talk, as though there was a reluctant hand squeezing the air from his lungs into his throat to enable him to form the words. "While Marcus is at work, the lady next door's keeping an eye on me, and the lady help comes in. So I'm well looked after, lass. No need to worry."

She sank on to the bed. Her head was down, her manner dejected.

"I know there's something wrong with *you*, lass. That's why you've come running to old Ernest, isn't it? Tell me."

"I don't want to burden you with my troubles."

"That's what I'm here for, isn't it?" He patted her hand. "Tell me."

They came pouring out, all the terrible things which, according to Faith Ringstead, Marcus had said about her. "I can't sing at the concert, Mr. de Verrier, I just can't face it. Now I know Marcus hasn't any faith in me any more, how can I have faith in myself?"

Ernest tried to pull himself up, but found it too much of an effort, so he sank down again. "You mustn't back out now, Carrie. It's the chance of a lifetime."

She was so immersed in her own troubles, she did not notice the high flush which had invaded his cheeks in his attempt to persuade her to change her mind.

"You can't lose your confidence now, lass. It's me you'll be letting down, you know. I've got my ticket and I'm going to hear you sing. You'll be up there on that platform, singing to me, just to me, Carrie, do you hear?"

She shook her head, but with less determination than before.

"Your parents –"

"My parents don't really care about me. If they did get upset about my not appearing, it would only be because the Ascott dress I'm going to wear wouldn't get the publicity my father's hoping for."

170

"Carrie," his hand reached out like fingers trying to find a light switch in the darkness, "not those parents, your real parents, the ones who loved you so much. Think of them, think of how proud they'd have been to know that their lovely little daughter had such a beautiful voice, she was given the chance to show it off on a concert platform in London." He saw by her eyes that he had struck a responsive chord. "And there's Marcus. You can't let him down, not after the way he's helped you."

"Marcus doesn't care about me any more, Mr. de Verrier. All those dreadful things he said about me –"

"You're not getting me to believe Marcus said anything of the sort about you. That woman made them up. I always thought she was poison. He loves you, Carrie –"

"Marcus *loves* me? You're so wrong, Mr. de Verrier."

"But he's kissed you. I've seen him do it myself."

"A man can kiss any woman who's willing, can't he? I was willing, so," she shrugged miserably, "he kissed me. He was never serious about me. He couldn't forget the past. Every time I went out with him I'm sure it was that other girl he was walking with, talking to, kissing, not me. He was only using me to get her out of his system. That day he came to see my parents, if he'd been really serious about me, he wouldn't have given in so easily. He hates my parents, Mr. de Verrier, he hates them so much he hates me, too."

"Don't cry, lass."

"I can't help it," she sobbed.

"Carrie," Ernest hoisted himself on to his elbow, "have you ever told Marcus the Ascotts adopted you?"

She recoiled at the suggestion. "I couldn't."

"Why ever not?"

"Because when I told Avery – I let it out unintentionally – he acted as though he'd been bitten by a snake. He treated me as if I had something horrible wrong with me. He couldn't get away from me fast enough."

"But Marcus isn't like that, Carrie."

171

"It's no good, Mr. de Verrier." She couldn't tell Marcus about the children's home, and the two people who came to choose her ... If she couldn't have his love, she certainly did not want his pity. "What difference would it make to his attitude, anyway? He would still look upon me as the girl with the background and the parents he despised."

Ernest sighed, suddenly weary. "Dry your eyes, lass. It'll all work out somehow. But don't you let me down, Carrie. You're going to sing at that concert as sure as I sit here, and I'm going to be there even if they have to take me in a wheelchair." His long white fingers, trembling a little, found her hand. "Promise me you'll go, you'll not let me down? Promise me, lass." His hand tightened, his voice held an overpowering urgency.

She sighed and capitulated. "I promise."

He sank back, smiling with relief, cheeks flushed, eyes staring and bright. "I'll see you," he said, "after it's over. I'll come round the back and find you." He pulled her down. "Let me kiss you, Carrie. A kiss for luck."

She bent down and he touched her cheek. Impulsively she returned his kiss, plumped up his pillows, made him comfortable and left him.

CHAPTER TEN

CARINA waited all day to tell Marcus she had changed her mind about the concert. At mid-afternoon she was called to his secretary's office.

"Mr. de Verrier has just telephoned," the girl said. "He asked me to tell you to rest at home tomorrow morning, and to rest your voice, too. He said he will call for you immediately after lunch and take you in his car to London."

So, Carina thought, he knew of her decision? His grandfather must have told him.

"I see." Carina frowned. "He hasn't been in today?"

"No."

"He didn't ask to speak to me?"

"I'm afraid not, Miss Ascott. He just told me to pass the message on."

"Oh. Thank you." She stood there, at a loss. "I suppose I might as well go home now."

"Good idea," said the young woman. "No point in staying."

No point, Carina thought, in doing anything. She had expected that the least Marcus would do would be to say how pleased he was that she had changed her mind, and give her some last-minute advice and encouragement.

She lay on her bed and listened to the afternoon silence. The housekeeper was out shopping. Phyllis was at one of her innumerable committee meetings and Lloyd was at work.

Out of the quietness her fears came knocking at the doors of her mind. They started with a tap like the noise of a woodpecker, growing into a thundering so loud as she thought about the ordeal in front of her that she turned on her front and covered her ears. Without Marcus, without his support and guidance, how could she face it?

But she would see him tomorrow. All the way to town she would be sitting beside him and then she would be able to draw reassurance from his confidence and strength from his strength. She should never have undertaken the assignment, she was not ready for it, she would make a terrible mess of the whole thing and Marcus would be ashamed of her.

She slept fitfully that night and awoke unrefreshed. The dress her father had given her was in a suitcase, having been expertly packed by one of the Ascott employees.

After lunch, when a car pulled up in the driveway, it was not Marcus who got out. It was Fleur Leeson. She was alone.

"Marcus sends his apologies, my dear," Fleur told her. "He's asked me to take you to the concert."

Carina did not seek an explanation. What was the use? Marcus had not bothered to come, but had acknowledged his responsibility by sending a deputy, a distinguished deputy, but it made no difference to the fact that he had not come himself.

While Carina went upstairs to flick a comb through her hair and put on her coat, she heard Fleur chatting to Phyllis.

"Marcus is a wonderful pianist," Fleur was saying. "He has had a very distinguished career. A year or two ago he was in constant demand as a soloist. In fact, he was quite a celebrity. Even now he performs occasionally in London and the provinces. He has a booking for a London concert coming along in two or three months' time. I believe it's being televised."

Carina, to whom this was news, heard it with a thrill of pride. She thought, with a wry smile, that it must be anathema for her mother to be forced to listen to such extravagant praise of the man she and her husband disliked so much.

"He's made a number of recordings," Fleur went on, "and has broadcast a few times with famous orchestras. You may have heard of him."

"Do you know," Phyllis commented in a trembling, excited voice, "when I heard the name de Verri-ay, I was certain I had heard it before!"

Carina opened her eyes at her mother's statement and was astonished by the power of suggestion. She knew, and her mother knew, that she had never heard the name until Carina became friendly with Ernest de Verrier.

Why, Carina wondered, as she pulled on her gloves, had Fleur taken it upon herself to act as Marcus's amateur publicity agent? Why was Fleur being so assiduous in her efforts to promote Marcus's image and provoke her mother to such rapture at the mere mention of his name?

"How terribly clever of him!" Phyllis was saying. "I really must tell my husband. Such an accomplished young man. And to have been so privileged as to meet him, too!"

And, Carina thought ruefully, to have been able to treat him so insultingly, to have been able verbally to have thrown him out of the house – and the family!

She joined the others and her mother kissed her warmly, saying she would see her after the concert.

"Now," said Fleur, when they were on their way, after extricating themselves from the tentacles of Phyllis's chatter and clinging arms, "I have received instructions from Marcus to talk to you like a Dutch aunt – I can't say 'uncle', can I? I've been told to talk to you as one professional singer to another."

"But I'm not a professional singer."

175

"After today you will be," Fleur replied confidently. "You will receive a fee for this performance and that is tantamount to making you a professional. You mustn't be so modest, my dear."

"I've never thanked you," Carina said, with a brave attempt to sound enthusiastic, "for securing this appearance for me. It was very kind of you."

Fleur made an expressive movement with her left hand. "It was nothing. I was so helped early in my career by others, I vowed that when my time came, I would help young artists, too."

"I hope I don't let you or Marcus down, Miss Leeson."

Fleur's hand touched Carina's arm. "Fleur, please. I have heard you sing, and I've heard Marcus's opinion of your ability. That is sufficient assurance for me to know that you won't let anyone down, yourself included."

"But I'm an unknown, and no one cares about unknowns."

"Now I know," Fleur laughed, "why Marcus said, 'For heaven's sake talk some confidence into the girl'! My dear, I'm a big name, so my public expects great things of me and heaven help me if I don't give them what they've paid to hear. My name would be mud amongst my fans and amongst the music critics next day. But you – you could, if necessary, get away with murder – not that you will give them 'murder'! You're young, new and appealing. They will admire you for all those things and more. They will, if necessary, forgive you for a great deal, because it will be your first appearance – we have mentioned that in the programme notes. Does that put your fears at rest?"

"A little."

"Good. You will go up on that platform and you will think to yourself, 'They are all human beings, many of them with their private problems and griefs. I can reach out and touch them just as easily as I did in the old days when I sang to the old people.' You see, Marcus has told me all about you."

Carina laughed, and even that was a relief from the tension that was binding her like tight bandages. "It helped me in those days," she said, "to fix my mind on one person. I always used to sing to Marcus's grandfather — you know him?"

"I have met him," Fleur replied.

"He's going to be there tonight," Carina told her.

"That's wonderful. You may not manage to see him, my dear, because, take it from me, so many people will be there the audience will seem a blur, but you sing to Marcus's grandfather, Carina. You just sing to him, whether you can see him or not, and forget all the others."

"I will," Carina promised fervently, "I will."

Carina changed into the dress her father had given her. It was pure Ascott, made of gold satin and covered entirely with a layer of gold lace. The sleeves were long, the neck scooped low and the skirt hung classically straight to the floor.

There had been a rehearsal that afternoon. Fleur had played the accompaniment to her songs. Had Marcus no intention of coming, Carina wondered in despair, had he delegated his role entirely to Fleur?

As her voice had echoed round the vast, empty auditorium, her achievement at being on the platform of a famous London concert hall felt hollow and meaningless without Marcus to share it with her.

Fleur had taken her for a light meal nearby. "We won't have much to eat," she had said. "It's not possible to sing well after too many helpings of food!"

Now the audience was drifting in and the tension was mounting. Still Marcus did not come. But Fleur had scarcely left her side. She had been wonderful, inspiring her, encouraging her, cheering her when she sensed her spirits were flagging.

"Marcus?" Carina had kept asking. "When is Marcus coming?"

"He'll be here soon," Fleur had assured her repeatedly, "he won't let you down."

Carina's performance was scheduled for the second half of the concert. Orchestral pieces occupied the whole of the first half.

During the interval, Fleur came to her again. She said, "Marcus has arrived," and watched the pale, tense face transformed with joy and relief. "Let me look at you. Make-up, excellent. Hair, beautifully arranged. Dress? Beyond description. Voice?"

Carina's hand went to her throat. "I think that's still working," she answered with a tight smile. "But Fleur, I'm terrified."

"Who isn't, Carina, at such a moment? I'm usually shaking in my shoes." At Carina's astonished glance she said, "It's perfectly true. Even hardened professionals suffer from last-minute nerves."

Then Marcus was there, beside Fleur, looking handsome in his formal dress. He, too, was every inch the professional.

"Marcus," said Fleur, "isn't your protégée beautiful?"

He eyed Carina narrowly. "Yes, she's beautiful." His voice was toneless, his face without expression. "The dress is magnificent. An Ascott creation, Carina?"

Carina, on the edge of tears, nodded. "Marcus," she whispered, "I thought you were not coming. What happened?"

He looked away. "I'm sorry. I was delayed."

Fleur cleared her throat, glanced at her watch and said, "You follow the item which is on now, Carina. Marcus, I hand her over to your capable hands. Treat her gently, won't you?" They exchanged glances. To Carina she said, "I wish you the very best of luck, my dear – and remember, you sing to one person, and that one person only. You promise?"

Carina nodded and watched her walk away like someone seeing a lifeline thrown to him fall short in a stormy sea.

Then Marcus looked at his watch. "A few more minutes." His manner softened a fraction. "Nervous?"

"Terribly. You're so lucky, Marcus. You know the ropes, you're an experienced performer."

"Take heart," his hand touched hers for a moment, "you're not really new to this yourself, are you? Remember the times you've faced an audience? Not as large as the one you will sing to today, but an excellent training ground for this sort of thing."

It was true, of course, she had been alone on stages and platforms many times, entertaining people. Although the level at which she had worked in the past was a very different one from this, it was a thought which did more to steady her nerves than all the last minute advice in the world.

He took her hand. "This way, Carina." Together they stood in the wings, listening to the cello solo which immediately preceded Carina's appearance. Marcus's thoughts were with the music coming from the stage, and as Carina studied his profile, even in the sparse lighting his face looked shadowed and heavy.

"Marcus," she whispered, "is there something wrong? You look so tired."

He held his finger to his lips, then his arm went round her shoulders and he smiled for the first time. "Don't worry about me. Relax, Carina. I'm with you now."

Although she knew he was following Fleur's advice and was being "gentle" with her, her heartbeats responded overwhelmingly to this touch of kindness.

"Your grandfather?" With a sweeping motion she indicated the auditorium. He nodded, and then she did relax.

The cellist bowed and withdrew. The applause died down.

"Now," Marcus whispered, gripping her hand, "follow me."

He led her on to the platform, bowed low to the audience and indicated to Carina that she should do the same. As the

179

applause rose and fell away expectantly, he pressed her fingers and moved to the piano.

The lights were lowered and the audience became a blur, a nebulous mass, as Fleur had warned her it would. It was impossible to pick out any individual, even her parents who, she knew, were sitting in the front row. She raised her eyes and looked towards the back, feeling that there, surely, must be Ernest. He always chose to sit at the back.

And that was where she directed her voice for the entire performance. She was singing to Ernest de Verrier more exquisitely than she had even sung to him before.

She sang an aria from Puccini's *La Bohème* and songs by Schubert and Tchaikovsky. The haunting, magical quality had returned with even greater poignancy and, because of the brilliance of Marcus's teaching, with a more profound effect than it had ever had in the past. She was reaching out to her audience, catching at their hearts and moving them to their depths as only she knew how.

When it was over the applause was tumultuous. Marcus left the piano and joined her, taking her hand. Together they bowed, acknowledging the applause. He pulled her close, whispered, "You were magnificent," and kissed her cheek. The audience loved it.

A child came on to the platform carrying a bouquet of flowers. Overwhelmed, Carina accepted it, kissing the little girl warmly. The card attached to the flowers said, in hand-writing she knew so well, "From Marcus, with love."

"With love." That was what he had said to her the day he had given her chocolates when they had come to London to hear Fleur sing. The words had meant nothing then, and they meant nothing now.

Nevertheless she whispered her thanks as he led her off at last. Fleur came hurrying back stage and hugged her. "You were wonderful, my dear, just wonderful. Such stage presence! She has it already, Marcus. It seems to come naturally to her."

Marcus left them, but Carina did not mind. The concert

180

was almost over and he would be waiting to bring his grandfather backstage.

Fleur accompanied her to the dressing-room and talked non-stop while Carina changed. When Phyllis and Lloyd appeared, Fleur withdrew discreetly.

They embraced her, called her the star of the evening and spilled over with praise. Others came in, people she had never seen before, congratulating her, wanting to shake her hand, take her photograph and have details of her life and career to date, her family and her thoughts of the future. They made much of the fact that she belonged to the wealthy Ascott family, and to Lloyd's delight, took pictures of her with her parents.

"Better than a full-page advertisement in a national newspaper," he whispered joyfully to his wife.

At last Fleur, who had been hovering in the background, rounded up the visitors and with great tact, urged them out of the room, leaving a flushed but triumphant Carina alone with her parents again. Her triumph, however, was tinged with defeat. Neither Marcus nor Ernest had come. The de Verrier family had turned their backs on her.

Her parents stayed on. It seemed they were waiting for her to leave with them. She supposed there was nothing else for her to do. No point in waiting any longer for a man who, after seeing her through her ordeal, had no more use for her. She looked for her coat.

There was a knock at the door and Marcus came in. Carina could not hide her joy – until she saw his pale face and strained manner. He apologised for interrupting and turned to go, but Phyllis said, with a coy, 'you remember me?' smile, "Mr. de Verri-ay? We have, of course, met before."

He turned to face her. He did not, however, return her smile. He bowed, rigidly polite, keeping his hand to himself, and Carina's heart sank at his intractable attitude, his implacable refusal to accept the Ascott olive branch.

Undaunted, Phyllis enthused, "We've heard so much

181

about you from your charming friend, Miss Leeson."

Then it was Lloyd's turn to pay a subtle compliment. "Read about your career in the programme notes. Very impressive, very commendable."

"You sound," Phyllis took him up, "such a wonderfully interesting person. I told Miss Leeson I was *certain* I had heard of you."

Marcus inclined his head, but remained unmoved.

"Our daughter did well tonight," Lloyd said gruffly. "We – er – must have a chat some time about her future. We should appreciate your advice, Mr. – er – de Verri-ay, er – Verri-er."

Carina had never heard her father so hesitant, so – for him – apologetic. Was this his way of asking forgiveness for their treatment of the young man who had come to their house, and at whom he had hurled unforgivable abuse? Her father, who apologised to no one, who demanded homage from all those he considered his "underlings"?

Whatever it was, it was lost on Marcus. He said briefly, "Her training will cost money."

"Money no object, old chap."

'Old Chap'? My word, thought Carina, he really has let Marcus into the 'club'. Was this Marcus's reward for his past achievements? If it was, it seemed Marcus wanted none of it.

"She will," Lloyd commented, "immortalise the name of Ascott."

"That," said Marcus laconically, with a swift glance at Carina, "remains to be seen."

"You've packed the dress, darling?" Phyllis asked, holding out her hand for the suitcase. "I'll put it in the car. We shall wait for you in the foyer. We must have a meal somewhere to celebrate, mustn't we, Lloyd, before we take her home?"

At last they had gone. Marcus had not moved from the door. A good place, Carina thought, from which to make a speedy exit should she start making emotional demands on

182

him. He could not have made his dislike of her parents more obvious. Now the concert was over, the end of their relationship, if such a word could be applied to their acquaintance, was near. He would not continue to act as her singing instructor.

"Carina?"

She did not look at him. Instead she took his flowers on to her lap and ran the tips of her fingers over the smooth surface of the transparent covering. "They're beautiful, Marcus. Thank you so much." She lifted her head. "Your grandfather? Was he pleased with my singing? Where is he? Why didn't you bring him in?" She put aside the flowers. "He surely isn't waiting outside all this time?" She started for the door, but Marcus blocked her way.

"My grandfather's not there, Carina. He was not – able to come."

"But, Marcus, he *did* come." Her eyes, large and a little rebuking, held his. "I *know* he was in the audience. I sang to him, all the time I sang to him."

"You may have sung to him, Carina," he spoke patiently, "but he was not there."

"What are you talking about?" Her voice rose as she tried to convince him he was wrong. "He was down there in the audience, urging me on. I could *feel* him, Marcus, so it's no use trying to fool me into believing he didn't come."

"I'm not fooling, my dear. He was *not* there. You know he was ill?"

She nodded. "Rheumatism, he said. It made him stiff. He had a chill."

"That's what he told you, because he didn't want to worry you, not at such an important time. In fact, the day before you saw him he had a heart attack – a slight one, slight enough to make him determined to overcome it and get to the concert hall."

"Come what may, he said," she whispered, "he would be there even if you had to take him in a wheelchair."

183

"He *was* recovering, Carina. It was sheer determination on his part. Nothing, he said, was going to keep him from hearing you sing. But last night he had another heart attack. He was rushed to hospital in the early hours. I went with him. He died this morning."

"No, Marcus, *no*!" She shook her head, refusing to believe him even now. "He *was* here, I *swear* he was here . . ." Tears spilled over and ran down her cheeks as she began to admit at last that Marcus was speaking the truth.

"Marcus," she cried, "oh, Marcus . . ." She reached out for him, but checked herself, covering her face. He hated her, he would not want to offer her comfort.

But he caught her as she stepped blindly away and gathered her into his arms, pressing her head against his shoulder and stroking her hair. She heard him speaking softly, tenderly.

"He *was* here, Carina, in your mind. You sang to him as he would have wanted. You came through the ordeal so well, he would have been beside himself with happiness. Think of that, Carina, only think of that. That's all he would have wanted you to do, not to mourn him."

He tilted her face and saw her eyes, those eyes which had attracted him, tantalised him and puzzled him so much in the past, but which were now streaming and desolate. "He loved you, you know. He looked on you as a granddaughter."

He held her close as she cried out her grief. Now and then there were voices outside in the corridor, a burst of laughter, a snatch of conversation, even a man singing. Then there was silence. At last the sobs that had racked her body lessened and died away and she stood still and silent in Marcus's arms.

"Carina," Marcus murmured, his cheek against her hair, "I was holding him when he died. Shall I tell you what his last words were?" She raised her head and he found his handkerchief and dried her tears. "He said, 'Tell Carrie you love her.' "

184

Her body stiffened and she whispered, "What did you say to that?"

"I promised I would. It made him so happy."

She caught her breath and there was accusation mingling with the pain in her eyes as she jerked herself away from him. "How *could* you make such a promise when you knew it wasn't true?"

"Is that what you think? Didn't you read the message on those flowers?"

"Of course."

"I sent them with my love. Did that mean nothing to you?"

"Your 'love'. It was understandable in the circumstances that you should add those words. People often do. They don't usually mean anything."

"Could they not have meant something this time?"

"What are you implying? That you *love* me?"

His fingers lifted her chin. "Is it so impossible?"

"Quite impossible. There's so much against it. You've said so time and again. Spelt it out, in fact. My background, my possessions, my parents . . ."

"I love you, Carina."

"You don't love me! And I know how to prove that you don't. There's something you don't know about me. When I tell you, you'll never want to touch me again. It's happened to me before, so I'll be ready for it." She moved out of his reach and took a deep breath for courage. She needed the courage because in a few moments the man she loved would be walking out of her life for ever. "I'm not what you think I am. I'm not really an Ascott at all. I'm an adopted child."

She waited for the recoil, the shocked surprise, the polite noises of sympathy. And the retreat. None came.

"My dear," Marcus said gently, "I know. My grand-father told me. He said he had promised to keep your secret until his dying day. I think he knew he didn't have long, Carina." There was a moment's throbbing silence. "So he told me. And, my love," he smiled, "you may be surprised

185

to know that I love you even more now, if that were possible, than I did before." He closed the gap between them impatiently and took her into his arms again. "And I *do* want to 'touch you again' – very, very much."

"But, Marcus," she looked into his face, bewildered now, "those awful things Faith Ringstead told me you said about me . . .?"

His eyes hardened. "Yes, I heard about those, too, from my grandfather. If I could tell you what I think of Faith Ringstead! She omitted – deliberately, of course – to tell you that I said some of those things – only some, my sweet, because the others she made up – when you first enrolled as a student, and before I began to know you properly. I can't understand how you came to believe her, or why you absorbed her poison so readily."

She clung to him. "I thought you hated me, Marcus."

He held her away for a moment. "*Hated* you? My darling, I've loved you for a very long time."

They stood for a while holding each other, then Carina asked, "Marcus, did Fleur know about your grandfather?"

"Yes. I told her when I asked her to deputise for me."

"And yet she agreed that I should sing to him . . ."

"Wasn't she right? Didn't the thought of him carry you through to the end?"

She whispered that it did.

"Which is what he would have wanted. Now do you see why I had to stay away from you until the last few minutes? I dared not tell you the truth until the concert was over. It would have shattered you."

She rested her face against him. He went on,

"When my grandfather told me you had been adopted by the Ascotts, it explained so many things about you that had puzzled me. For instance, your difference in looks and manner from the rest of the family, those words you wrote to Seth's music, which were not just an exercise of the intellect but which so obviously came from your heart. Then there was your love of music, instead of your sharing

186

the family's total ignorance of it. There was your exquisite voice, your beautiful eyes which tormented me because I couldn't understand the sadness and uncertainty they held."

He whispered, "I was appalled to hear how you had been orphaned, and the terrible circumstances of the crash." He kissed her passionately and murmured, "I'm crazy about you, Carina. You're my life, do you know that?" He looked at her face as if he were reading a book. "You're compassion," he kissed her eyes, "you're love," he kissed her lips, "and here," his hand rested against her breast, "you're provocation . . . and desire . . . and a deep, sweet peace."

"And I," she whispered back, "cannot tell you how much I love you. I can only show you."

"And what, my darling, could be better than that?" He kissed her again as if he never wanted to let her go.

But the moment came when he had to tell her reluctantly that they must come down to earth. "My parents are staying with me for a while. This time you'll be meeting them as their future daughter-in-law."

She caught his hand. "Will they be glad, do you think?"

"Glad? They'll be delighted! They've been hoping for it for months, ever since they met you, in fact." He put her hand to his lips. "You know we have some obstacles to overcome, my sweet?"

She smiled. "For 'some' read 'two', my parents."

"Your adoptive parents, yes. We may have a fight on our hands, you realise that?"

"I'm not so sure, Marcus. Fleur was wonderful. It was almost as though she knew about us and was trying to promote your image to my mother."

He laughed. "To 'sell' me, you mean? She did know about us, because I told her, so she probably was."

"You could tell by the way they spoke to you this evening that she made a 'sale', Marcus. You're a celebrity in their eyes now, and that, to them, is almost as good a recommendation in a prospective son-in-law as a fortune!"

He laughed again. "Well, we'll see. But whatever their

187

reaction may be to our engagement, *you are marrying me.*
Is that clear?"

"Yes, Marcus," she answered, her face radiant.

"Right, my darling." He took her hand. "Together we'll meet the foe. Then I'm taking you home – my home – where you belong."

Why the smile?

. . . because she has just received her Free Harlequin Romance Catalogue!

. . . and now she has a complete listing of the many, many Harlequin Romances still available.

. . . and now she can pick out titles by her favorite authors or fill in missing numbers for her library.

You too may have a Free Harlequin Romance Catalogue (and a smile!), simply by mailing in the coupon below.

Have You Missed Any of These
Harlequin Romances?

All books are 60c. Please use the handy order coupon.

PP